# A CANDL

Young Sister Bryony Clemence and the new surgical
registrar Grant Stirling rub each other up the wrong
way whenever they meet, but is it only chance that
dictates that they should meet so often?

# A CANDLE
# IN THE DARK

BY
GRACE READ

**MILLS & BOON LIMITED**
London · Sydney · Toronto

First published in Great Britain 1982
by Mills & Boon Limited, 15–16 Brook's Mews,
London W1A 1DR

ISBN 0 263 74078 1

Set in 11 on 12½pt Linotron Times


03/1182


Photoset by Rowland Phototypesetting Ltd
Bury St Edmunds, Suffolk
Made and printed in Great Britain by
Richard Clay (The Chaucer Press) Ltd
Bungay, Suffolk

# CHAPTER ONE

THE Royal Heathside Hospital, in a fashionable suburb of London, was the epitome of excellence in modern medicine. Its structure of polished black stone and gleaming chrome rose to an impressive height of twelve storeys, contrasting sharply with the small shops and streets of quiet Victorian houses on its doorstep.

At first there had been some protests when this giant started to rise in the neighbourhood, but during the ten years since its completion the locals had grown proud of their new hospital. There were 700 beds in spacious and well-equipped wards and the very latest technology in all supporting departments. Added to that, a thriving Medical School and an efficient School of Nursing . . .

'Why, it's almost a pleasure to be ill these days!' So said Mr Lomond to Dr Stirling, the stalwart new registrar, on his first visit to Addison Ward.

The patient slipped his arm around the trim waist of young Sister Bryony Clemence. 'They're a great bunch of nurses on this ward, Doc, but she's the cream!' He grinned at her embarrassment as she eased herself away. 'You don't need to blush, Sister.'

The houseman, John Dawson, accompanying Dr Stirling, winked broadly at Bryony, but the registrar, concentrating on the charts he was studying, either did not hear or chose to ignore the remarks.

He glanced towards Mr Lomond, on Addison for the control of his diabetes, and observed pleasantly:

'Well, you seem to be stabilising nicely now. You'll be going home before long.'

The small group moved on towards their last patient, but before discussion could begin both doctors' bleeps sounded urgently. Making for the nurses' station John Dawson picked up the telephone. After a brief exchange he came speeding back to murmur urgently to the registrar: 'It's a cardiac arrest, Simpson Ward.' Whereupon both he and Grant Stirling were gone in a flash.

Student Nurse Patty Newman, fresh from the Introductory Block and full of enthusiasm, dogged Bryony's footsteps. 'Does that mean we have to get a bed ready, Sister?'

Bryony smiled at her eagerness. 'No, the patient will go to Intensive Care first . . . if they're in time.'

She adjusted a white hairclip holding the frilly cap on her honey-blonde curls and glanced at her watch as an orderly appeared pushing the patients' tea-trolley. 'Well, I expect that's the end of rounds for this afternoon. You can relieve Nurse Smith while she goes to tea, Patty. She's in High Dependency, with Tina. You know, the new anorexic girl.'

The junior sped off to her appointed task while Bryony detailed others of the staff to go to tea.

The doctors' round had been later than usual that

afternoon, with Thursday clinics having been extra busy. Normally it was fairly quiet on the ward at this time of day, patients being occupied with visitors, and now that the doctors had gone Bryony was able to arrange for a certain Royal Heathside tradition to be observed.

With one of their staff nurses due to leave the hospital that day, there had already been a celebratory get-together with senior Sister McCullagh during the lunch-break. Having a discreet word with some of the remaining nurses, Bryony suggested that now would be a suitable time for carrying out those 'last rites' in the bathroom.

'Mind you don't get her watch wet!' she murmured with a grin, 'and Jean, you stay on the nurses' station in case anyone buzzes.'

She herself returned to the office. At four-thirty Sister McCullagh would be back on duty. Meantime there was quite a bit of writing to catch up on for when Bryony handed over for her days off.

Absorbed in her work the return of Dr Stirling caught her by surprise as he drummed with his fingers on the glass of the open door.

'Oh, hallo! I wasn't expecting you back today,' she said pleasantly.

He inclined his shapely dark head in the direction of the bathroom. 'Some kind of horseplay going on along there?'

His disapproving tone of voice piqued her a little. She explained levelly, 'One of our staff nurses is leaving today. She's getting the traditional ducking, that's all. But I assure you the ward isn't being neglected.' Her clear blue eyes met his, quite un-abashed.

'I see. That's one practice they didn't indulge in at my previous place.'

His condescending half-smile had her gritting her teeth and counting to ten before she replied: 'Well, most hospitals have their lunatic customs. Have you come to finish the round?'

'Not unless there's anything worrying you. I came to have another word with that youngster we admitted yesterday – the anorexic girl.'

'Tina Vincent.' Bryony flicked through the Kardex sheets.

The registrar thrust his hands into the pockets of his white coat and half-seated himself on the desk as Bryony came round to join him. 'We had great difficulty in persuading her to be admitted. Barely five-and-a-half stone and she was insisting there was nothing wrong with her. Has her mother been in touch?'

'Yes, Mrs Vincent came in last night. She actually seemed relieved that Tina isn't to be allowed visitors yet. I had thought she might be incensed.'

Grant Stirling adjusted his long stride to keep pace with Bryony's light steps as they made their way towards the four-bedded unit reserved for patients needing close observation. 'I'm not surprised . . . some parental problems there I gathered.'

They reached the unit and as Bryony entered she pulled up sharply, her inside lurching. Only three of the beds were occupied. Where the sixteen-year-old patient should have been there was now only Student Nurse Patty Newman straightening the empty bed.

'Nurse, where's Tina?'

Patty self-consciously fastened a gaping button on her pale blue uniform. 'She's gone to the toilet, Sister.'

'Oh dear!' Bryony bit her lip in vexation. 'She's on complete bed-rest, and that means bed-pans. You should have buzzed for assistance. Didn't Nurse Smith explain to you about not letting Tina leave the ward?'

'We-ell, yes, she did.' The junior looked embarrassed. 'But Tina pleaded with me . . . I didn't think it could do any harm.'

With a resigned sigh Bryony despatched Patty to bring the patient back to bed, mentally deciding to have a talk with the junior about the difficulties of handling anorexia nervosa.

She turned to the silent and straight-faced Dr Stirling and made an attempt to excuse the girl. 'Sorry about that. It was lack of experience I'm afraid. This is her first ward and she was relieving for Tina's duty nurse.'

'So the girl has probably had her fingers down her throat to make herself vomit.' He spread his hands in a gesture of exaggerated forbearance. 'Oh well, I suppose we can always start again from square one.'

He turned his back on her while they waited, exchanging a brief word and a smile with another of the patients in the ward. Bryony glared at his broad shoulders and handsome dark head and decided the man was a positive Jekyll and Hyde, the way he could turn the charm on and off at will. A pity his bedside manner didn't extend to his relations with the staff! She wondered how far it would get him with Tina; anorexics were notoriously difficult patients to deal with.

Patty Newman came back with her strong young arm supporting the wraith-like teenager. Lank dark hair framed what would have been an attractive, elfin face, had it not been for its gaunt pallor and the apathy in the lack-lustre brown eyes.

Tina glanced at the doctor uncertainly, propping herself against the side of the bed for support.

'Hallo, young lady. And what have you been up to?' Grant Stirling's deep authoritarian voice was severe. It sent an unwilling tingle down Bryony's spine but seemed to have scant effect on their patient.

She flung him a suspicious glance and returned insolently: 'What's all the fuss about? I told you, there's nothing wrong with me. I only fainted because I'd been rushing. And then this idiot passer-by has to call an ambulance.'

'And you, my dear, should be extremely grateful to that idiot, or you wouldn't be feeling quite so perky as you are now.' The registrar folded his arms and fixed her with a look that allowed no argument. 'Back into bed with you. We need to have a little talk about one or two things.'

He nodded dismissively to Bryony and the junior. 'You carry on . . . I'll buzz before I leave.'

'Crumbs!' muttered Patty Newman with an apologetic glance at Bryony as they left doctor and patient together. 'I'm terribly sorry, Sister, if I put my foot in it.'

Bryony shrugged. 'Oh well, no real harm done. You can't be expected to know all the pitfalls to begin with. Come with me to the office and I'll tell you something about Tina's illness while we've got a moment.'

She went on to explain the need for a strict regime if they were to win the battle against the girl's determination to starve herself. 'But it's also essential to build up a good relationship with her. We have to give her confidence that we really are on her side. There's usually some underlying factor which triggers things off. In Tina's case it may be because her parents are divorced. One thing's for sure, she's going to resist our efforts to fatten her up. And remember that these patients can get awfully clever at finding ways of disposing of their food.'

Nurse Newman was a little on the plump side herself. 'Fancy having the willpower to starve yourself!' she sighed, 'I've only got to see a doughnut and I'm sunk.'

Bryony laughed. 'This is a *compulsion*, not willpower. You thank your lucky stars you've got a healthy appetite.'

Searching in a tray on the desk she found a duplicated set of notes, citing a previous case history. 'Here you are, Patty, this will give you an over-all picture until we have time for a proper teaching session. And now you get back to the nurses' station before His Nibs buzzes, or he'll think we're absolute rubbish on this ward.'

The traditional 'last rites' had been duly fulfilled Bryony found when she looked in at the bathroom. The doused staff nurse was climbing into a dry pair of jeans and a sweater which someone had provided in readiness.

'That was freezing,' she giggled. 'If I catch pneumonia you won't be getting rid of me after all. I'll be back on the ward before you know it. I wouldn't mind, either,' she added, 'if all MO's were as dishy as Stirling.'

'You must be joking!' Bryony scoffed. 'He's not my cup of tea.'

At her elbow, Patty Newman interrupted, 'Excuse me, Sister, but Dr Stirling is asking for you . . . and Nurse Smith is back from tea now, so what shall I do?'

'You can write up your Kardex,' said Bryony as she made to return to the High Dependency area.

She found Grant Stirling speaking with Nurse Smith just outside Tina's bay. Turning a kindly smile in the direction of his patient, he said: 'So long, Tina. I'll see you again,' before he drew Bryony along the corridor out of sight.

'That child has no idea how sick she is,' he confided, his expression one of deep concern for the girl.

'Neither has her mother,' Bryony replied. 'I had the impression she finds it all something of a nuisance.'

'The glucose drip we gave her in Casualty has given her a false sense of well-being for the moment,' Stirling went on. 'We'd better have another blood test and some X-rays to eliminate any other possible factors. I've explained to her about the privilege system,' he added as they walked along to the office to complete the necessary forms. 'Definitely no visitors yet, Sister, or phone calls. I've promised that as soon as she starts to gain weight on a regular basis we'll let up on the routine. You know the drill, don't you?'

Bryony nodded. In spite of the hostility he'd aroused in her she could not help but admire the man for his dedication and thoroughness. She found herself wishing, not only for Tina's sake, that there would be a satisfactory outcome to his prescribed course of treatment.

'Your Nurse Smith seems to have the right idea,' he went on, 'cheerful and friendly without being soft.'

It was comforting to know that *one* of the staff actually met with his approval. 'Yes, Smith's a good nurse,' Bryony said. She added reflectively, 'Tina makes us all feel sad. I mean, a girl of that age should be full of beans and enjoying life . . .' She broke off, all at once aware of his eyes assessing her. Grey-green eyes they were, with flecks of amber, and an expression in them she couldn't quite fathom. She flushed. Perhaps she'd been jabbering on too much; perhaps he thought her opinions of little consequence. And then she decided it didn't matter what he thought when there were things to be said which might have a bearing on Tina's illness.

'When I was speaking to Tina's mother,' she continued, 'I got the impression she's a very career-minded person but determinded to do her duty. She considers this is just a slimming craze which has gone overboard.'

'Amazing!' murmured Grant Stirling, half to himself and still regarding Bryony with critical eyes.

'What is?'

'The length of those eyelashes.' It seemed more like a clinical observation than anything else. It left her nonplussed as he seated himself at the desk and filled in the forms for X-rays and blood test, after which he replaced his pen in his top pocket and, with a brief nod, went on his way.

Bryony was still pondering whether his remark had referred to her eyelashes or Tina's. And she thought he'd been listening to what she had to say about the patient! In a state of utter perplexity she didn't quite know whether to laugh or ex-plode.

With Sister McCullagh's return to the ward it was a welcome relief to Bryony to go off duty. Her exchanges with Grant Stirling had left her feeling peculiarly ruffled and disconcerted, although she knew it was illogical to let him bother her unduly. In an odd way, despite his brusqueness he fas-cinated her. She couldn't quite figure him out.

Seeking to dismiss the annoying registrar from

her mind she stopped for a coffee at the busy canteen in the reception area on the ground floor of the hospital. Her flatmate Judy had gone home for her day off, so there would be no-one to talk to back at the flat.

It was barely a month since Bryony had been promoted to the position of junior sister on Addison Ward and she was not yet completely at ease with the burden of responsibility it carried. She supposed she would get used to it in time. Judy, on the other hand, was still quite content to staff on Casualty. Accidents and emergencies were a familiar pattern to her now and she seemed thrive on urgency.

'Besides which,' she had crowed, 'no beds to make, no bed-pans, no boring charts to keep.'

'But you don't ever really get to know your patients,' Bryony had countered. She preferred the 'real nursing' as she put it, feeling there was nothing more gratifying than seeing people return to health. But then, she and Judy were totally different temperaments, which was probably why they had been such good friends all through their training.

With Judy there was always some new enthusiasm to enliven the scene. It was good for them both, Bryony realised. It stopped them carrying their work worries home with them.

'If you're to survive in this job,' Judy declared, 'you have to live a full life of your own.' And she made it her business to see that they did.

Standing at the counter waiting to be served

Bryony pondered on her friend's latest bright idea. She jumped as warm hands grabbed her waist from behind and a soft beard nuzzled her cheek.

'How's my favourite girl?' a voice murmured in her ear.

Turning, Bryony found herself looking into the lively, impudent face of anaesthetist, Mike Tavistock.

'Oh, hi, Mike,' she returned, smiling.

'What were you thinking about with that faraway look in your eyes?'

'As a matter of fact, I was trying to think of something beginning with a "P" that I could wear to a party. Any ideas?'

'Whose party is that?' demanded Mike.

'It's another one of Judy's ideas, for our Hallowe'en gig. She thought it would make a change from witches and whatnot if we all dressed up as something beginning with "P". Although why "P" don't ask me.'

He considered for a moment. 'Mmmm . . . how about . . . pregnant?'

Bryony grinned. 'You're a great help. I don't think I fancy carrying a cushion around with me all evening. It would be a trifle restrictive on the dance floor.'

He gave it some more thought, stroking his neat dark beard. 'I could be a pirate.'

'Who said you were going to be invited?'

'I don't need to be. Where would your parties be without me? And speaking of invites,' Mike went on as they carried their drinks to a vacant table, 'would you like to come with me to Phinny's "At Home"?'

Bryony stopped stirring her coffee to stare at him. 'You mean . . . *our* Sir Phineas?' she said at length.

'What other Phinny do you know? He's a one-off.'

He was indeed. Bryony always felt considerably in awe of Sir Phineas Forbes, despite the occasional twinkle in the bird-bright eyes of that senior and much respected consultant.

'He said to bring my lady,' Mike went on.

'I'm not your lady.'

He regarded her impishly. 'We can soon alter that.'

'Oh, Mike!' She curbed a smile. 'I like it the way we are . . . I'm not joining your harem.'

'Right, so that's settled.' He yawned and stretched expansively. 'The old boy worked us like dogs today. Thank God he's retiring at Christmas.' Leaning forward, he urged, 'You will come, won't you? I promise you it'll be a rave-up . . . Phinny's quite a lad in his own way.'

'You haven't said when it is, or where.'

'His place in Kensington, on Saturday. It's rather grand. There'll be good eats. Phinny always hires people to do the catering, being a bachelor.

'Okay,' Bryony agreed, warming to the idea. 'I'll count it as part of my education.'

'Pick you up about eight, then.'

Mission accomplished, Mike sauntered off, leaving her wondering exactly what she was in for and trying to make up her mind what to wear for such an occasion. One thing was for sure, a party at Sir Phineas Forbes' Kensington mansion would be nothing like Judy's Hallowe'en 'P' party.

Smiling to herself Bryony gathered her cloak around her shoulders and set off, out of habit, in the direction of the car park. Halfway there she paused, remembering. She had left her car at the garage that morning for its MOT. They hadn't phoned to say it was ready, so it would have to be the bus home.

With a groan of annoyance she retraced her steps, making for the bus-stop outside the main entrance. She saw a bus disappearing into the distance and after waiting for five minutes decided that she might as well walk to the next stop as stand about. It was a mild autumn evening and she could probably reach the heath by the time another bus came along.

The wide open spaces of the heath with its little hills and vales and scattered trees were always an attraction to Bryony. It reminded her in parts of some of the country around her Devon home.

That was one of the advantages of working at a place like the Royal Heathside, she mused as she stepped out. You had all the advantages of London and all the pleasures of the green belt too. She and her friends had spent many happy hours on the heath during their hard-up training days, and many a budding romance had flourished listening to music in the open-air concerts.

Arriving at the edge of the heath where the traffic

intercrossed, Bryony waited at the lights for the road to clear. To her great annoyance another bus sailed by.

'Damn!' she muttered, mournfully gazing after it. That meant another fifteen minutes to wait, unless she carried on walking.

As she stood hesitating a sleek silver car pulled up alongside her and the passenger door was pushed open.

'Can I help you, Sister?' a familiar voice enquired, and she found herself being addressed by the new registrar.

At that moment even Sir Phineas himself would have been a welcome sight to Bryony. Her feet were aching and the night was closing in. She didn't really fancy walking the rest of the way. The heath could be spooky after dusk; there were often odd characters about.

'Oh, thank you, Dr Stirling,' she exclaimed gratefully. 'Would you be going towards the station?'

'I'd make it my business to even if I were not,' he snapped, motioning her to slide in beside him.

Smoothly the car moved off again, the registrar's strong, capable fingers resting lightly on the wheel.

'Do you always walk across here?' he queried.

It was ridiculous the effect his voice was having upon her. There was a fluttery feeling in her throat. She had to draw a conscious breath before answering, 'No, I usually drive, but my car is out of commission at the moment.'

He flung her an unsmiling glance from beneath

his straight dark brows. 'Well, until you get it back I should think you would be advised to be less stupid and find yourself some alternative means of transport.'

Bryony turned surprised blue eyes to gaze at him. She swallowed, determined not to get rattled. 'And what do you mean by that?' she asked, quietly controlled.

'I should have thought that was obvious. You should have more sense than even to consider walking alone after dark in a place like this. Unless, of course, you wish to end up carved to pieces in the bushes.' His tone was disparaging. 'Last night we admitted a young woman who'd been savagely attacked somewhere in this area.'

They had arrived at the station now and he pulled up. 'Will this do you . . . or can I take you any further?'

She felt like an erring schoolgirl, slapped down. Her colour mounted. 'This will be fine. Thank you for your concern,' she added with studied politeness. 'By your book perhaps I was also stupid to accept a lift from someone I hardly know.'

He seemed taken aback for a moment. Then his eyebrows shot up in mild amusement. 'Yes, maybe you were. We can't afford for our staff to take risks. Especially . . . the cream, didn't our patient say?'

With lips twitching he leaned across to assist her as she fumbled with the door handle. His face was barely inches from hers. She noticed the healthy outdoors glow of his skin, more like a sportsman than someone who spent his time with the sick. His breath came pleasantly warm on her cheek as he said 'Goodnight!'

Inwardly fuming she slammed the car door and covered the short distance down the side road to the flat in record time.

A light shone out from the downstairs living-room of the old Victorian house, the bottom half of which she and Judy shared, and as Bryony entered the hall her flatmate hailed her cheerfully.

'You're back early,' Bryony called, flinging her cloak and her cap on her bed before joining her friend to hear about her day.

Judy came from the bathroom with a towel wound turbanwise around her wet chestnut locks. 'How do you like this?' She gave a twirl in her new brown velour housecoat. 'It's from my mum—a pre-Christmas present. She always buys things well in advance and can never hang on to them,' she chuckled.

'Oh, that's gorgeous.' Bryony tried to show en-thusiasm but she was still seething with vexation. Flopping on the sofa she kicked off her shoes and let out a heavy sigh.

'So what's eating you?' Judy asked.

Bryony scowled. 'That man!'

'What man?'

'His Lordship—Grant Stirling.'.

'Oh, him. A real pin-up, isn't he? I haven't had much to do with him yet, but the duty nurse for his clinic the last day I was on said he was great to work with. Why, what's he done to get under your skin?' asked Judy with mild curiosity.

Bryony shrugged. 'Well, nothing really, I suppose, except to give me a lift home. But it's his general attitude. I seem to rub him up the wrong way, and he certainly does me, the self-opinionated, sarcastic brute.'

'Oh dear! Sounds like a really lovable guy,' laughed Judy. 'Now you couldn't say anything like that about John Dawson, could you?'

Bryony remembered the wink of the hard-working, conscientious young houseman whom they had both known for some time. 'Oh no, John's great.'

'Glad you approve, because that's why I'm back early. He rang me up at home, and he's taking me to a show tonight. I shall have to get a move on.' Judy trailed back to the bathroom, rubbing at her hair.

Bryony went back into her bedroom to change her uniform for jeans and a sweater before searching the refrigerator for something to eat.

'There's only eggs,' she called out. 'Are you eating with John as well, or shall I do you some scramble?'

'Yes please, we shan't have time for a meal.'

'That's all of three times you've been out with John. Must be getting serious,' Bryony sang out.

Judy came back to plug in her hair-dryer, looking extremely pleased with life. 'Could be! What about you, are you doing anything tonight?'

'Nope.' Bryony cracked eggs into a basin and measured in some milk. 'But I do have a very interesting date for Saturday,' she boasted, beating her mixture.

'Oh, what's that?'

'Just a little "At Home" at Sir Phineas Forbes' Kensington place.'

Judy was saucer-eyed. 'Who's taking you to that?'

'Good old Mike.'

'Mixing with all the top brass these days, aren't we?' Judy teased. 'I can see I shall have to get myself a sister's post.'

'Oh, I don't know,' Bryony made a face, 'sometimes I think it would be nice to be a third-year again and let someone else have all the hassle.'

Her friend hooted. 'Oh, come on! Face the finals all over again? No, thank you. I say, I wonder if your pet aversion will be at Phinny's party? Perhaps it's in his honour, to integrate him with the firm.'

'Don't say things like that!' Bryony wailed, 'I was actually beginning to look forward to it.'

# CHAPTER TWO

AFTER searching through her wardrobe and finding nothing suitable for the élite occasion ahead, Bryony spent her day off on a shopping spree in the West End.

'Will I do?' She spun around on her high-heeled strappy sandals, displaying her new outfit, when Mike called to collect her on Saturday evening.

His eyes approved her slim figure beneath the sheer black chiffon with its off-shoulder flounced neckline. 'Wow! Shan't have you to myself for long in that,' he breezed. 'It's a good thing you girls wear uniform for work or the cardiacs would be dropping like flies.'

Judy came from the bathroom in her dressing-gown, having promised herself an early night after a heavy day. She put her head on one side, admiring Mike's velvet jacket and silk shirt. 'I haven't seen you looking so expensive for ages, either. What it is to move in exalted circles!' she exclaimed in mock envy.

'All right, Jude,' Bryony laughed, 'you know very well you wouldn't swap places with anyone at the moment. You did say I could borrow your fur jacket, so as not to let the side down, didn't you?'

24

Her friend spread her arms magnanimously. 'Feel free! What's mine is yours . . . barring my guy, that is. I'll get it for you.'

Returning with the soft grey chinchilla jacket, she draped it around Bryony's shoulders, said: 'Enjoy yourselves,' and retired to her room.

'Nothing but champagne for me in this lot,' quipped Bryony as they made their way down the cracked cement path of the old house to where Mike's Spitfire was parked in the road.

'Oh, you'll get champagne all right.' He opened the car door for her, making a long-suffering face. 'I shall have to go steady myself, as I'm driving.'

She chuckled. 'Sorry about that.'

They joined the maelstrom of Saturday night traffic speeding towards London's West End. It took them rather longer than Mike had anticipated to reach Sir Phineas Forbes' residence, one-way traffic systems not helping, but at last they arrived in the fashionable Georgian square. Solidly-built opulent mansions sat behind neat iron railings in a broad sweep around the central gardens.

Mike managed to squeeze his car into a parking place and, taking Bryony's arm, led her towards the steps of Sir Phineas's home.

Their ring on the bell above the polished brass plate was answered almost immediately by a man-servant.

'Please join Sir Phineas upstairs when you're ready,' he told them, after indicating rooms set aside for cloaks.

With the majority of guests now assembled, a pleasant hum of conversation arose above the strains of tinkling piano music. Bryony and Mike ascended the graceful curving staircase to the balcony, their feet sinking into the rich plaid carpet which covered polished treads. The gilded wrought-iron balustrade was an intricacy of metallic flowers and leaves.

'Is he a millionaire?' murmured Bryony, pausing wide-eyed to take in the ornamented ceiling and priceless oil-paintings on the walls. 'I didn't realise medicine was so profitable.'

'Don't I wish it were, sweetheart,' Mike growled. 'All this in inherited family loot, I believe. He's got quite an impressive write-up in *Who's Who*.'

In the doorway of the reception room at the top of the staircase stood Sir Phineas himself, silver-haired, resplendent in tartan kilt and dress jacket.

'M'dear fellow, delighted to see you,' he boomed, pumping Mike's hand. 'Ah, yes, we have met,' he recalled as Mike introduced his partner. 'You look charming, my dear.'

'Thank you.' Bryony smiled, his warmth making her feel more at ease. She extended her hand. 'I hope you have a good evening, Sir.'

'Och, we'll not stand on ceremony!' Sir Phineas bent his six-foot-three to plant a kiss on her cheek. 'Now off you go and enjoy yourselves.'

'He's actually quite human, isn't he?' Bryony sipped the champagne they were handed. 'I'm surprised he remembered me.'

'Oh, he remembers all the pretty ones.' Mike scanned the gathering and raised his glass to a group of familiar faces across the room. 'Who shall we honour with our presence?'

The anaesthetist was a gregarious type and Bryony knew that she might well see little of him once he got circulating. Not that she would mind. Theirs was an agreeable friendship with neither being possessive about the other.

'There's Grant Stirling, over there.' Mike's eyes narrowed with sudden interest, '. . . and who do you suppose is that smashing bird he's with? Not one of ours, is she?'

Almost as soon as she had entered the room Bryony had been aware of Grant, standing head and shoulders above those he was with. She had quickly turned the other way as his gaze wandered in her direction. Now she threw a casual glance over her shoulder towards the girl in question, an attractive redhead in a striking emerald green satin trouser suit, who seemed to be holding Grant's attention.

'No, I don't know her,' Bryony said.

'Pity. Looks like they've been cornered by Sister Matlock and her old man. He's not a bad guy, but that woman monopolises every conversation. Shall we rescue them?'

'You can if you want to. There's Prof Baxter from Haematology over there, looking a bit lost. Think I'll go and talk to him.'

'Okay. You know plenty of people, don't you? See you around.'

While Mike wandered over to try his luck with the redhead, Bryony joined Professor Baxter and admired the rose in his buttonhole. It was a hobby of his, she discovered, breeding roses, and he delighted to tell her about his efforts at cross-pollination. She reflected for the umpteenth time what odd mixtures people were.

A hot buffet was being served by neatly-uniformed waitresses before Mike searched her out again. In the meantime she hadn't lacked for company.

'Sorry if I've neglected you, sweetheart,' he said. 'You know how it is . . . eyes across a crowded room and all that.'

Bryony grinned and tucked into her portion of delicious moussaka. 'Your eyes ought to be permanently crossed, the number of times that happens to you.'

'Now, now!' he cautioned. 'Not that I got very far this time . . . the way Stirling's sticking to that girl you'd think they were glued together. Her name's Vivien. Gorgeous, isn't she?'

'It's a good thing I'm easy-going,' teased Bryony. 'How many more of your women would be as accommodating as me while you rave about someone else?'

He devoured a chicken vol-au-vent. 'Oh, you haven't been doing so badly yourself, I noticed.' Wiping his mouth on a paper napkin, he kissed her lightly on the nose before strolling off to speak with someone else.

Despite being drawn into lighthearted banter

with other friends standing nearby, she had an uncanny feeling that she was being watched.

Compelled to glance round, across the room her eyes met the steady gaze of Grant Stirling. His expression was one of either pity or reproach, she wasn't sure which. And she felt a sudden desire to explain to him that she and Mike were merely friends, that he was free to flirt with whom he pleased, and that she didn't mind a bit. But it was no business of his anyway, she told herself angrily.

She deliberately started an animated conversation with the chief radiologist who seemed only too flattered to be singled out for her attention.

The general atmosphere had been somewhat starchy to begin with, but tongues were gradually loosening and reserves yielding to the festive atmosphere. Coffee and liqueurs were being served when the Dean of the Medical School took it upon himself to propose a vote of thanks to Sir Phineas and to regret his forthcoming departure from London.

Sir Phineas kept his response brief. 'You're all here to enjoy yourselves, not to listen to speeches,' he declared. 'As soon as the buffet is cleared away we can start to liven things up.'

'Oh no, not party games!' muttered Professor Baxter in Bryony's ear, 'He had us actually playing blind man's buff once.'

But apparently it was to be dancing at first. A small band had arrived and they set up their equipment near the piano. Tables were pushed back, rugs rolled to one side. The two large communicating rooms provided a sizeable dancing area.

'Everybody on the floor now . . .' Sir Phineas raised his voice in command as the music started up. 'We want no shrinking violets,' and seizing the laughing red-haired Vivien by the hand, he swung her into the dance, his kilt swinging.

Mike returned to claim Bryony. He was an excellent dancer and she loved the way he whirled her around. Grant Stirling was partnering an elderly nursing officer, to her obvious delight, and Bryony couldn't help reflecting that it was rather a courteous gesture on his part.

Having got things moving to his satisfaction, Sir Phineas next coerced them all into a progressive Virginia Reel. After reminding them of the steps he announced '. . . and upon taking leave of your partner to move on, you do so with a kiss. Defaulters will pay a forfeit!'

There were no defaulters. This unexpected frivolity had them all in good spirits. As Mike had said, the private Sir Phineas was a surprisingly different person from the public one, Bryony decided.

With these thoughts going through her head as she exchanged a kiss with the shy Professor Baxter and moved forward, she was startled to find herself alongside Grant Stirling.

'Good evening!' he greeted her, capturing her hand in a warm grasp.

Her heart, irrationally, began to thump. 'Oh, hallo!'

'May I call you Bryony?'

'Please do . . . that's my name,' she returned, jokingly.

'I wondered if I'd been singled out for your cold shoulder tonight?' He glanced down at her with a satirical expression as they went through the sequence of the dance.

'Why should you think that?' She was annoyed to find her colour rising as she spoke, besides being disturbed at the turbulent feelings the touch of his hands on her body aroused. 'Anyway, there was nothing to prevent you coming to speak to me,' she countered.

'With all those admirers dancing attendance on you? As a newcomer that would have been putting my foot in it, wouldn't it?'

She didn't answer as he guided her through the final steps. Her agitation mounted as the moment of parting drew near. He was going to kiss her . . . but it would probably be just a perfunctory, dutiful peck. Nevertheless there were butterflies in her throat as he murmured: 'Well, we must do as Sir Phineas wishes, even if it is against your inclinations.'

Bryony offered her cheek. 'Half measures?' he said, turning her face to his, his eyes glinting with mischief. Then he took full possession of her mouth for far longer than was necessary. When he finally released her she was so angry she could have hit him. Curbing a smile at the fury in her eyes he passed her on to the next in line.

She found she had come back again to Mike, who appeared to be in a state of utter bliss. 'God bless

Phinny!' he greeted her. 'I actually got to grips with the delectable Vivien. She's peachy!'

'And he's an unspeakable rat,' said Bryony between gritted teeth.

'Who? Grant? Why, what's he done, trodden on your toes?' He nuzzled his soft dark beard against her face and said, soothingly, 'Never mind, Mike won't let you down.'

She recovered her good humour and laughed. 'I'd like that in writing.'

The reel came to an end and they exchanged prolonged, affectionate kisses, only to be interrupted by a polite cough from the man-servant who came to summon Mike to the telephone. After taking the call he returned, looking thoroughly disgruntled, apologising to Bryony: 'Here we go . . . I'm wanted in theatre. Sorry love, I'll have to abandon you. No problem about your getting home, though. I bumped into Stirling and he's offered to give you a lift.'

'Oh, Mike!' Bryony wailed, 'I'd have preferred to make my own arrangements.'

'Well, the guy offered, I didn't ask him. Anyway,' Mike winked, 'do me a favour and see if you can find out what's between him and Vivien.'

It was well past two a.m. before the company finally broke up after some riotous party games between dances, finishing with a rousing session of the Gay Gordons and Auld Lang Syne.

Despite Mike having to leave early, by deliberately putting distance between herself and Grant, Bryony managed to enjoy the rest of the evening.

But now, as goodbyes were being said, she felt more or less obliged to approach him before going to collect her jacket.

'Mike said you'd offered to run me home. It's awfully kind of you, but not to worry. There are plenty of people going my way.'

'It's no trouble, is it Grant?' chimed in Vivien agreeably. There was a fascinating Scottish lilt to her voice. 'He can drop me off at St Benny's first and then go on with you.'

Hands in his pockets, Grant raised an indulgent eyebrow. 'There you are, it's all arranged. Well, I'll wait for you in the hall.'

There seemed no more to be said. Bryony took her leave of Sir Phineas before going downstairs with a crowd of others. In the cloakroom she was joined by Vivien who began chatting to her in a friendly fashion.

'Are you nursing at St Benedict's?' Bryony was encouraged to ask.

'Yes. I'm in my first year there.'

It surprised Bryony that Dr Stirling should condescend to date a first-year student, lovely though she was. 'Was that where you met Grant?'

'Oh no, I've known him—we-ell, a long time.' She didn't attempt to explain further and Bryony felt she could hardly press the point.

They made their way back to the hall where Grant waited with other escorts. 'Ah, there you are!' Tucking an arm under each of theirs he led them out to his car.

Seated in the back, Bryony thought she was

bound to feel awkward while the two in front chatted with the ease of their long-standing relationship. But Vivien made a point of including her in the small-talk, turning round and plying her with questions about the Royal Heathside, comparing it to the smaller, older hospital of St Benedict's. All the same, she couldn't help feeling a twinge of envy at the obvious affection existing between the two in front.

Arriving at the nurses' hostel of St Benedict's Grant left the engine running while he slipped out of the car to walk Vivien across the forecourt.

'Bye!' Vivien called with a sweet smile and a swift wiggle of her fingers towards Bryony. 'Perhaps we'll meet again sometimes.'

'Yes . . . I hope so.' She couldn't help warming to this friendly, outgoing girl, but since Grant's social circle and her own were unlikely to overlap, meeting Vivien again seemed a remote possibility.

Returning quite soon, Grant opened the car door on Bryony's side and motioned her to the seat in front. She could scarcely do otherwise than sit beside him as directed, but she was glad that they hadn't much further to go.

'What a great party,' she remarked, determined to keep the conversation going on a civilised basis. 'I was always a bit wary of Sir Phineas . . . until tonight.'

'It's not people like Sir Phineas you need to be wary of,' was his cryptic rejoinder.

She presumed that remark might be directed at

Mike, but decided to ignore it. 'Did you know Sir Phineas before you came here?'

'Oh yes, I've known him, we-ell, a long time.'

Oddly, that was precisely what Vivien had said about Grant, it occurred to her.

'And how long have you been at the Heathside?' he wanted to know.

'I trained there. But I've only recently become a sister. I still find it rather intimidating at times.'

A crooked smile twisted his mouth. 'I don't get the impression you're a timid lady. Quite the opposite in fact.' He cast her a sideways equivocal glance.

'No, I'm not timid in that sense. I meant the job, the responsibility; it takes some getting used to. Oh, you know what I mean.'

'Yes, but I'm sure you're going to cope admirably.' There was a hint of patronage in the teasing tones.

Pompous prig, she thought. He wasn't worth wasting effort over. Directing him to the side road and to her flat, she thanked him for the lift and bade him a brisk goodnight to put paid to any possible ideas he might have had of being asked in for a nightcap.

But in spite of being physically tired sleep was to prove elusive to Bryony that night. Her brain was hyper-active with thoughts of Grant Stirling persistently plagueing her. 'Oh, damn the guy,' she muttered, turning and thumping her pillow yet again. At least his softer attitude towards Vivien showed that he wasn't totally woman-proof. And she couldn't forget that kiss. True, on his part it had been no more than a touch of devilment during the Virginia Reel, but its effect on her had been tantalising, despite her objections. She fell asleep with the thought that it might be quite an experience to be kissed by Grant if he really meant it.

Being on early shift Judy had already left for work before Bryony surfaced on Sunday morning. In the living-room by the telephone she found a note from Judy saying:

'Your mum phoned – will ring you again tonight.'

'It conjured up a picture of her family and the comfortable old grey-stone farmhouse in the Exmoor village that had been their home for generations. Immediately she felt cheered as she made coffee and went about having her bath.

She could almost smell her mother's home-baked bread and see the dogs stretched out on the rug in front of the Aga in the kitchen, the cat curled up in the sun on the window-seat.

Her mother's last letter had told her about the Harvest Festival and various bits of village gossip. Her father had also added a postscript saying be sure to let him know what train to meet at Exeter when she came on leave. He always insisted on paying her train fare, not liking to think of her driving all that distance alone.

There had also been a scribbled note from her young sister Joanne who had confided that she was in love with Tony, a boy from a neighbouring farm.

Joanne had been in and out of love with a number of boys quite regularly since turning fourteen.

Bryony was glad they were all such good correspondents. Judy's mother, for instance, lived not too far away which made telephoning simple and inexpensive. They had no need to write to each other. It was much nicer receiving letters, Bryony always thought. Besides which, when you lived at a distance going home for time off was much more of a treat then when you could pop home on the bus.

In anticipation she checked her diary for the date of her long weekend to be tacked onto the few days holiday still owing to her. Next weekend it was their 'P' party, but the weekend after that she would be on her way home to see them all. She did wonder why her mother had phoned but concluded that it was probably just to confirm the date of her visit.

Addison Ward was remarkably peaceful when Bryony presented for duty at one o'clock that day. Four patients had been discharged and only two admitted since her days off. And with early and late shifts overlapping in the middle of the day, for once the staff were not working at pressure.

'We've got Mrs Phillips, seventy, with a fractured neck of femur—they were full up in Osteo.' Sister McCullagh giving her report smothered a sneeze with her handkerchief. 'And there's Colin Goddard, nineteen, epileptic, query brain tumour,' she went on, describing their two new patients.

'I've come across Colin before,' said Bryony,

looking thoughtful. 'Query brain tumour. Oh dear, I hope not. He's a nice kid.'

Sister McCullagh sneezed again and Bryony peered at her with a frown. 'You don't look too good. Why don't you go off? We're not pushed, are we?'

'I think I will if you're sure you don't mind? I shouldn't be spreading my germs around here.' Smothering yet another sneeze, Sister McCullagh dabbed at her sore nose. 'You will see that all the patients are back in bed before visitors, won't you, dear? Oh, and I promised Nurse Smith she could do the drugs round—she wants to get her Drugs Assessment. But make sure there's a reliable person keeping an eye on Tina Vincent . . . don't want all our good work undone when she's beginning to co-operate . . .'

Bryony laughed and urged her senior towards the door. 'It'll be all right. Don't worry. Everything will be done just as you like it. And I can always ring the nursing officer if we need help.'

As soon as Sister McCullagh had gone on her way Bryony went to have a personal word with the two new patients. She then proceeded to make sure that the work of the ward was progressing. Temperatures were recorded, fluid charts checked, beds straightened and patients all comfortably settled before their visitors came in.

This time a wiser Patty Newman was sent to sit with Tina while Nurse Smith, under Bryony's supervision, administered the prescribed drugs.

With the round completed and the drugs trolley

safely locked away behind the nurses' station, Bryony sent Patty Newman for Mrs Phillips' X-rays, just in case they should be needed.

And so the time passed smoothly with all routines faithfully observed and a generally calm and orderly atmosphere on Addison Ward.

When the nurses had written their Kardex notes on their own particular patients, there was even time for a teaching session on epilepsy, with particular reference to their new patient.

'In Colin's case,' Bryony told the girls gathered around her in Sister's office, 'red and green lights seem to trigger an attack. That makes life very difficult when you think of traffic lights. Even watching TV can affect him. Lately he got so depressed he stopped taking his Phenytoin, which led to the fits increasing. He's to have an EEG tomorrow, in case of a brain tumour. He'll probably have a brain-scan too. Meantime we'll control the fits with drugs. It may be simply a question of getting him stabilised again.'

A phone call from John Dawson broke up the session. Orthopaedic now had a bed, he rang to tell them, and would they please transfer Mrs Phillips.

Sending the late-shift nurses for their tea-break, Bryony stayed behind to make the necessary transfer arrangements before taking her own break.

Down in the canteen she ran into a theatre staff nurse dashing for a quick cup.

'God knows when we shall finish tonight,' the girl groaned, 'we've just had a red alert. Lorry jackknifed into a bus or something. I should be off at four-thirty. Supposed to be going to a PTA meeting tonight. My little girl's not going to be too pleased.' She gulped her drink and ran.

Bryony remembered that Judy also should be off at four-thirty. If things were as bad as the theatre nurse had predicted, most likely Judy, too, would get caught up in the action.

Her thoughts were confirmed later that evening when Judy phoned Addison Ward around seven o'clock, sounding weary.

'You've got three vacant beds, Bry? Right, will you take three casualties for us . . . we've filled all the surgical vacancies.' She went on to describe the patients. 'It's a man and two women whom Stirling's not happy about. Only cuts and bruises, but they're all a bit shocked . . . need a bed for the night at least.'

'Okay,' Bryony returned, 'Send them up, we'll be ready,' and she alerted the staff to make preparations.

Fortunately work on the ward was well ahead. Patients' suppers had been served and cleared away. Washings and pressure areas could wait until the last of the visitors departed at eight o'clock.

The first of the accident victims arrived in a wheelchair, together with his notes. He was a stocky man of fifty, badly cut around the face from flying glass, but no bones broken, although he was obviously distressed. He was also rather chesty, so they propped him up in bed in one of the single rooms, making him as comfortable as possible and

showing him where to press the button should he
need attention.

'Your wife has been contacted, Mr Gladwin,'
Bryony reassured him. 'I expect Doctor will be up
to see you again later. And this is Nurse Newman
. . . she will look after you.' With the arrival of the
other two patients she left Patty Newman to complete Mr Gladwin's temperature chart.

One woman with a badly lacerated leg gave no
trouble, but the other with only minor abrasions
was inclined to be hysterical. When both had been
assigned to nurses and attended to, Bryony closed
the ward on the last of the lingering visitors.

Going to her office she dealt with the paperwork.
There was always a great deal of clerking to be done
for new patients, even if they were only to be
admitted for a short time.

By eight-thirty her writing was finished and she
was able to return to the ward to see if any nurse
needed help in settling her patients for the night.
Satisfied that all were as comfortable as possible,
treatments carried out and toilet needs attended to,
she made a final check on the two new women
patients before crossing over to the male section.

The slight figure of young Colin Goddard came
ambling back to his bed from the direction of the
toilets. His gait was a little unsteady, Bryony
thought, and she paused to help him off with his
dressing-gown, folding it up and replacing it in his
locker.

'Feeling all right, Colin?'

'Yes, Sister. A bit of a headache, that's all.'

She straightened the covers as he climbed back into bed. 'I'll get the night staff to give you something.'

Picking up his sketch-pad that had slipped to the floor and knowing that he had been to art school, she asked: 'May I look?'

'Sure!'

The pad was full of amusing cartoon-like drawings of nurses and patients. Bryony chuckled as she looked through. 'Do you want to be a cartoonist?'

'It's all I'm any good at, but it's not easy to get in.'

She came to a more detailed drawing which was an excellent likeness of Patty Newman. 'This is great . . . you should sign it and give it to her.'

He smiled shyly. 'Oh no, I want to keep that.'

At that moment Patty Newman herself came hurrying towards Bryony, her face stark with panic. 'Sister!' she hissed urgently, 'It's Mr Gladwin . . . he's gone a dreadful colour . . . he can't breathe!'

# CHAPTER THREE

BRYONY sped with Patty Newman to the sideward to find the patient gasping painfully, his face ashen, his lips blue.

*My God! He's going to crash!* was her immediate reaction.

Outwardly calm but with her stomach churning, she felt for his pulse. It fluttered feebly beneath her fingers. His pallid skin was clammy. There were beads of sweat on his brow. There was no time to lose.

'Phone for the arrest team, quickly,' she ordered Patty, who shot off like a rocket towards the nurses' station.

Meanwhile Bryony had pressed the emergency buzzer which, at the Heathside, was by every bed to summon prompt assistance.

'All right, Mr Gladwin,' she said in a firm voice, 'we'll soon have you more comfortable.' Rapidly she wound the bed flat and whipped away the pillows.

Others of the staff had by now arrived in answer to her call for help. She rapped out orders, sending them scuttling for the cardiac-arrest box, airways, re-breathe bag, drugs, and prayed that the arrest team would arrive soon.

By the time that Patty Newman had returned to

assure her that the team was on its way, Bryony could find no pulse and Mr Gladwin had stopped breathing. Exerting all her strength she applied a two-fisted thump to his chest and began to massage the heart.

'What shall I do?' murmured a staff nurse at her elbow.

'Put in an airway and apply the re-breathe bag,' panted Bryony, carrying on with her massage.

Oh, where was that arrest team? Why didn't they come?

In fact it was only minutes before the experts did arrive, but to Bryony it seemed like eternity before Grant Stirling pulled her to one side. She could have wept with relief to see him.

Following closely on his heels were John Dawson and Mike Tavistock with their scientific equipment.

Grant fixed up the heart monitor. 'There's no rhythm . . . we'll have to de-fibrillate,' he decided swiftly. 'Got the pads, John?'

His colleague connected the electrical apparatus to the patient's chest. Grant prepared to give the first charge.

'Stand clear everyone.'

After several attempts the quavering heart began to steady. 'He's responding,' John said, with a degree of satisfaction.

'Adrenalin, Sister!' Grant clicked his fingers impatiently. Bryony had anticipated the request and put the syringe into his hand instantly. He glanced up in mild approval.

Life began slowly to return to the patient, his colour to improve. Holding his limp hand Bryony squeezed it between both of hers, murmuring: 'Don't worry, Mr Gladwin, you're going to be fine.' And she wondered if there had been a faint answering pressure.

After setting up the drip solution Mike Tavistock taped the needle into place in Mr Gladwin's arm. 'So the Royal Heathside wins again,' he said cheerfully. 'Well, you won't need me any more. I've done all I can do here and there's another heart I've got a date with.'

Putting an affectionate arm around Bryony's shoulders, he gave her a hug before collecting his equipment and taking himself off.

Bryony glanced at her watch. It was by now ten p.m. She had been briefly aware of the night staff coming on duty when one of them had popped her head in and whispered that the patient's wife was waiting in the visitor's room.

Now she said to Grant Stirling: 'Mr Gladwin's wife is outside. May she come in . . . or will you have a word with her first?'

Grant continued his close observation of the patient. 'His pulse is improving now . . . he's looking better.' He straightened up. 'Yes, I suppose I should see her first and then she can come in for a few minutes. We'll have to get this guy along to Intensive Care as soon as possible though, John. I'll leave that to you.'

He followed Bryony through to the waiting room where she left him to explain things while she herself made a cup of tea for the distressed Mrs Gladwin.

The remaining day staff had gone off duty by the time Bryony was able to give her belated report to the night staff nurse.

Afterwards, going along to the ward kitchen for a much needed drink for herself, she was met by Grant who had returned to the ward in search of his stethoscope.

'The perfect Dr Stirling actually *forgot* something?' she had an impish desire to remark, but out of politeness and because she was feeling happy about Mr Gladwin, all she said was: 'Would you like some coffee?'

'Thanks. That would certainly be welcome.' He parked himself on a chair looking generally rather satisfied with life, if a trifle weary.

She busied herself at the stove. 'I hear you had a bonanza down in Casualty this afternoon.'

He ran a hand over his slightly dishevelled thick brown hair. 'Yes, it was pretty gory. One should get used to it, but one never does.'

Passing him his drink, she sat down facing him and purely for something to say, said: 'You hail from Australia, I hear.'

There was veiled amusement in his grey-green eyes. 'The grapevine works very well here. Yes, I'm from down under.'

'You don't sound particularly Australian.'

'That's because my parents were English. And I spent a number of school holidays over here.' He spooned sugar into his mug and stirred. 'We don't all go around calling people "Sport" and saying "fair dinkum".'

She grinned. 'I suppose not. My experience is limited to TV and Rolf Harris.'

Feeling self-conscious under his scrutiny she lowered her eyes and ventured: 'Is Mr Gladwin going to make it?'

'Possibly. If your reactions hadn't been so prompt he wouldn't have had a chance. You did well there. I said you would cope, didn't I?' The grey-green eyes were still assessing her when she stole a look at him. 'Shouldn't you be gone by now?' he went on. 'I hope you're not contemplating walking home again.'

She gave a light laugh. 'Of course not. As I said, my car was laid up that night. I've got it back now. I'm not completely irresponsible you know.'

He took a sip of his coffee, continuing to look at her over the rim of the mug. 'No, I'm sure you're not. What puzzles me is why you bother with a chap like Tavistock. Sure, he's fine at his job. But I hadn't been here five minutes before it was obvious that he's the Heathside Casanova.'

Bryony felt her hackles rising. How *dare* he abuse one of her friends. She glared at him.

'Then if you haven't been here five minutes surely you shouldn't be making snap judgments, should you?' Her tone was frosty. 'Mike may give the impression he's a great ladies' man but underneath he's okay. And I think my friends are my concern, not yours.'

The previously agreeable atmosphere vanished.

Thunder-faced he set down his half-finished drink. 'That puts me in my place. We seem destined to disagree outside of professional matters.'

'Let's stick to those then, shall we, Dr Stirling?' She sounded calm enough but inside she was boiling.

'Suits me.' Abruptly he rose and made for the door.

'Don't you want this?' She waved towards the stethoscope which he had left on the table, inwardly chalking up a point to herself. Not that she felt any great triumph when he snatched it up and departed without another word.

'Damn you, Grant Stirling!' she muttered to his disappearing back.

It was well past eleven p.m. by the time she reached the flat. Judy was still up, lounging in her pyjamas on the sofa, endeavouring to unwind by watching the late-night film. She switched off the television to listen to Bryony's account of the ward drama.

'Oh yes, that was the nice old boy we sent up to you, wasn't it?' she remembered. 'Glad he didn't collapse on us; we had enough on our plate as it was. By the way, you missed your mum again. She rang about ten.'

Bryony looked at her watch. 'Too late for me to ring back now, they'll all be in bed. Was it anything special, did she say?'

'Something about an old school friend of your father's . . . his son's a doctor and your folks have invited him for a weekend. They thought it would be nice if you could meet up and travel down together. Might be interesting?'

Bryony made a dubious face. Her clash with Grant Stirling had left her with a jaundiced view of doctors for the moment.

'Anyway, she said she'd write because they'll be out for the next couple of evenings,' continued Judy. She went on to extol the virtues of Grant Stirling in his handling of their rush of casualties . . .

'One firm word from him and no bother from anyone. I reckon he's the best registrar we've had in years. I hope there'll be someone like him around if ever *I* need emergency treatment. If I weren't in love with John I might even be batting my eyelashes at him.'

Bryony had been about to voice her own entirely opposite opinion of the man, but in the face of Judy's unstinting praise her own quibbles seemed rather petty. After all, she had no fault to find with his professional conduct, and apart from his criticism of Mike – whom she had to admit did ask for it at times – Grant's only crime was to rock her equilibrium. She concluded it was just a clash of personalities, and so she limited her remarks to saying that he had certainly done a good job for Mr Gladwin.

Changing the subject she talked about their forthcoming 'P' party. 'I've settled for being a palmist. All I'll have to do is rig up a gypsy costume, get some big gold ear-rings and one of those triangles trimmed with coins for my head. I can do the palm-reading bit as well; I read it up once for a local fete we had at home. What about you, Judy?'

'Oh, Mum and I decided I could be a pussy cat. She's making me a black velvet cap with ears and a tail to pin onto my black leotard.'

Judy started giggling. 'We thought John could be a pupil from St Trinian's and wear my old school gym-slip. Good job my mother's a hoarder.'

She went on to say that everything was arranged for the party to be held in the doctors' messroom, which was in a separate building at the rear of the hospital. It was a favourite place for social functions with the advantage of being convenient for those on standby duty.

Bryony yawned. 'Well, it's bed for me. I'm early turn in the morning.'

Feeling considerably more cheerful after their gossip she took herself off to the bathroom. Judy's bubbling high spirits had helped to push less pleasant matters to the back of her mind. But it was only a temporary respite. No sooner had she settled down in bed and switched off her reading lamp than she began reliving the events of the evening.

The exasperating registrar, who seemed determined to cross swords with her whenever they met, would not be dismissed from her mind. She couldn't help contrasting his kindness in dealing with Mrs Gladwin to his curt exchange with herself in the ward kitchen.

With most people Bryony got on well enough. And it wasn't that she wished to quarrel with Grant Stirling. In an odd sort of way she even found him attractive. Recalling the pressure of his mouth on hers at Sir Phineas's party, a little thrill went down her spine. She found herself contemplating yet again what it would be like to be properly kissed by Grant Stirling.

And the very idea of that wrecked all possibility of sleep. Switching on her bedside lamp again Bryony took up a magazine and read until her eyelids drooped.

The alarm startled her into wakefulness the following morning. She silenced the bell quickly so as not to arouse Judy, who was not on until later.

After taking a quick shower Bryony put on a clean dark blue uniform and fastened the silver-buckled belt around her trim waist. Breakfast was a hurried bite of toast and a mug of coffee before climbing into her car and setting off for the hospital. She thought it almost certain that Sister McCullagh would be off duty again, with the severe cold that she had. Bryony sent up a fervent plea to the Almighty that the day would be crisis-free. The previous day's trauma had been quite enough to be going on with.

Her prayer, however, was not to be gratified. Up on Addison Ward she found all the staff gathered in Sister's office in a great state of consternation.

The nursing officer, also present, greeted Bryony's look of enquiry with a heavy sigh. 'Good morning, Sister Clemence, I'm afraid you've walked into trouble here.'

'It's Tina Vincent,' the night staff nurse explained, raising her eyes ceilingwards. 'It's been

one of those nights! Colin Goddard had another fit
. . . Mrs Morris pulled out her drip . . . we turned
our backs for five minutes and Tina disappeared,
the stupid girl!'

Bryony frowned. 'Disappeared? How could
she?'

The nursing officer spread her hands and confes-
sed herself mystified. 'We've looked everywhere!'

'I know she was in bed just before six this morning,' one of the nurses piped up, 'because I spoke to
her when I took a bedpan to someone else.'

'And it just isn't possible at night to have someone sitting with her all the time.' The staff nurse
chewed at her thumb-nail. 'I hope to goodness she
hasn't done anything crazy.'

Bryony tried to think logically. 'She can't have
gone far without her clothes.' She went to a cupboard in the office and looked. 'Well, they're still
here. I suppose she *might* have slipped out in her
dressing-gown, but that would have made her conspicuous. You've tried the toilets?'

At that moment the telephone rang on the
nurses' station and a junior was sent along to
answer it. Returning, she said, 'It's Tina's mother,
asking for you, Sister.'

They all exchanged glances.

'Okay, switch it through here,' said Bryony.

After speaking with Mrs Vincent for some moments she replaced the receiver with a sigh of relief.
'Breathe again, everyone. Tina's turned up at her
home. Apparently she borrowed a coat from the

locker of the woman in the bed opposite. *And* some money for her bus fare!'

'Well, thank heaven for that,' said the nursing officer. 'Now I've heard everything! And what's the other patient going to say?'

Bryony smiled wryly. 'Her mother's full of apologies and she's bringing the stuff back later in the day. She says Tina is so much better anyway that it's pointless her being here, and I couldn't persuade her otherwise. I don't know what Dr Stirling will have to say to that,' she went on with a sinking heart.

The nursing officer scratched her head. 'Oh, we'll have to sort it all out later. I'll notify the office. Meantime you have a wardful of other patients to look after.' She left them to it.

While the night staff nurse gave her report to Bryony others of the day staff helped to get patients sitting up for the breakfast which was about to be brought round. With plenty of work to do the day staff had little time to spare in worrying over their self-discharged patient. But when washings, baths and beds were finished, and treatments given and medicines dispensed, there was a certain amount of speculation during coffee breaks.

'Seeing that she's discharged herself, Sister,' Patty Newman pondered, 'supposing she got worse, would we take her back?'

'If we had a bed we would. She's still a very sick girl, Patty,' Bryony explained, 'and she is only sixteen. It's her mother's duty to bring her back, or at least consult her own doctor. Actually, we are empowered to make her come back since she's endangering her own life. But I don't know that it would accomplish much, not without her co-operation.'

'I'm jolly glad it was the night staff she skipped out on and not us,' put in Nurse Smith. 'At least we can't be blamed.'

That was true, but even so Bryony dreaded Grant Stirling's appearance on the ward that afternoon. She prepared herself for some scathing criticism, but when he discussed the matter with her in the office, after rounds, he proved remarkably restrained.

'Well, anything's liable to happen in these cases,' he said, showing little surprise.

'What do you propose to do about it?' Bryony asked. 'She's far from out of the wood yet, isn't she?'

Sprawled in his chair, long legs stretched out in front of him, Grant gazed into space, running his pen absently through his fingers. 'That's the problem . . . compulsion gets you nowhere . . .' he began, when Bryony had to interrupt him.

'Just a moment,' she warned as a well-built, smartly dressed woman approached and hesitated in the doorway. Bryony stood up. 'It's Mrs Vincent, isn't it? Come in. This is Dr Stirling. I'm sure he'd like a word with you.' She placed a chair for the mother who seated herself nervously on the edge of it.

'I really must apologise for Tina, skipping out like that without a word to anyone,' the woman said with a short laugh. 'And fancy taking liberties with someone else's coat! I told her she should have asked for her own things or she'd have people thinking she was a thief.' She nodded towards the small suitcase she had brought. 'I've brought it back . . . it's not damaged, and I've brought the lady some chocolates to make amends.'

Mrs Vincent paused for breath, glancing uncomfortably from one to the other. 'Tina's put on quite a bit of weight, she tells me. I'm sure she's going to be sensible about eating after this. Shall I take her own clothes now?'

Grant Stirling leaned forward in his chair and fixed his stern gaze upon her. 'Mrs Vincent,' he said, in quiet tones, 'do you want your daughter to die? Because she may well do if she doesn't come back and continue her treatment.'

The woman's mouth sagged. 'B-but . . . she's only a bit thin. You know what young girls are, think they're fat if they can't get into a size ten. Her father always used to call her "Fat", that was his name for her,' she remembered, laughing. 'Before he left us, that was. Of course, in those days she was a bit plump. He used to tease her that she'd end up well-upholstered, like me. I-I think that was what started this slimming craze. It was all his fault.'

'Never mind whose fault it was,' Dr Stirling continued. 'The danger weight for a girl of your daughter's build is six stone. Tina is five-and-a-half. She is listless, anaemic, unable to concentrate, and unless you help us to help her, you might as well kiss her goodbye.'

They were brutal words but they had their effect, as also did Grant Stirling's forceful personality, Bryony was aware.

Mrs Vincent licked her dry lips and swallowed. 'D-do you mean that, Doctor? You're not just trying to frighten me?'

'Madam,' he returned, glowering, 'I am in the business of medicine, not horror movies.'

She looked suitably chastened. 'Oh yes, I know . . . I'm sorry. Well, I'll do what I can to talk some sense into her, but she's very obstinate.' She heaved an enormous sigh. 'Daughters! Give me sons any day. My boy has never been the slightest trouble. He's at university now. She could go if she put her mind to it. She used to be bright enough, but will she stay on at school to take her A's?' Mrs Vincent shook her head.

Bryony gently interrupted the outpouring. 'As Dr Stirling says, at present Tina finds it very difficult to concentrate on anything. If she were a more normal weight, say eight stone at least, she'd have a different outlook. You can't expect much of her in her present state of health.'

Grant Stirling rose to his feet. 'I trust you'll try to bring her back as soon as possible. We'll keep the bed available as long as we can.' With a brief, autocratic nod, he went on his way.

Watching his departure, Mrs Vincent shrugged her solid shoulders and made a wary gimace, albeit with a certain grudging admiration in her eyes. 'I don't envy anyone who gets on the wrong side of *him*,' she said.

'Dr Stirling is very concerned for your daughter,' Bryony defended. 'He's disappointed at the outcome. You will try to persuade her to come back, won't you? I know it won't be easy, but I'm sure you can do it.'

'It would certainly suit me better to have her here being looked after for the present,' the woman grumbled. 'I've got a demanding job to hold down. I'm supposed to be going up North for a conference in a few days. It's very tiresome.'

Bryony went to the cupboard to bring out Tina's own clothes and exchanged them for the coat which Mrs Vincent had brought back.

'And here's the fifty pence she helped herself to, and the chocs for the lady. You will tell her how sorry I am, won't you? I'll tell her myself if you like,' Tina's mother offered.

'That's all right. She's a little poorly, we can't have her worried,' Bryony explained, 'but I'll give her your message at a suitable moment.'

When Mrs Vincent had gone Bryony went about her work feeling unusually depressed. Although she had not been personally involved in Tina's flight, it worried her to feel that Addison Ward had, in a sense, failed the youngster. But the behaviour of anorexics, she reminded herself, was always unpredictable. Even so, she couldn't help feeling that despite his few words the registrar was displeased. And some of that displeasure could easily rebound back on her. It was a disturbing thought.

# CHAPTER FOUR

THE remainder of that week seemed set to carry on in the same unsatisfactory pattern.

With Sister McCullagh still off sick with her cold Addison Ward was provided with a relief staff nurse to help out. While the extra pair of hands was welcome, the girl's bossy know-all attitude was a continual irritation to others on the ward and at times Bryony had her work cut out to keep the peace.

Mrs Vincent telephoned to say that Tina could not be persuaded to return. 'But there's always plenty of food in the house,' she said, 'I can't do more than provide the best for her. I sent her to the doctor, but our own GP's on holiday and she didn't want to see his locum.'

'Didn't you go with her?' Bryony asked.

'I couldn't. I have to go to work.'

'Oh dear, that's a pity. Someone should really be keeping an eye on her. I should take her again yourself if you possibly can.'

The woman made a half-hearted promise and Bryony put the phone down, shaking her head in despair.

She reported the phone call to the registrar and houseman when they arrived for rounds that afternoon and Grant Stirling said he would arrange for a social worker to visit.

He struck a further regretful note by reporting the outcome of the brain tests on their young epileptic, Colin Goddard. 'There's a rapidly-growing tumour,' Grant said. 'The neuro man has pronounced it inoperable, so I see no point in transferring him to that department. He may as well stay here with you where he knows every-one.'

Bryony felt a tug at her heartstrings. 'How long has he got, can you say?'

The registrar stroked his long straight nose. 'Possibly a matter of weeks, although it's useless to make forecasts. We'll put him on radio-therapy to relieve the pressure; otherwise there's not a great deal we can do except to make him as comfortable as possible. I'll write him up for diamorphine for when the pain gets bad.'

They moved out of the office to begin their routine checks on other patients.

Passing Tina's empty bed at the close of the round. Bryony sighed: 'I wish that girl had parents as caring as Colin's.' It reminded her that she would not be on duty when Colin's parents came to visit that evening and she certainly did not wish the news to be broken to them by the relief staff nurse. 'Will either of you be available to see his folks this evening?'

Grant Stirling readily agreed. 'Sure. Ask some-one to ring through and one of us will come.'

Outside the lift John Dawson rang the bell. 'Got your cossy all ready for this party on Saturday then, Bryony?' he breezed.

'What party is this?' enquired Grant.

'Oh, it's just a fancy dress get-together for Hallo-we'en,' she explained dismissively.

'It's in the doctors' mess. Look in, Grant, if you're not doing anything,' invited John.

Inwardly Bryony groaned, wishing John hadn't mentioned it. She would almost certainly spend most of her time with Mike. He was always good for a laugh and she felt the need to relax completely after the cares of the ward. She could do without the disapproving eye of the registrar following her around, making her self-conscious with his air of moral judgment.

Grant Stirling neither said he would or he wouldn't be looking in. He merely allowed himself a laconic half-smile as the lift arrived and bore the doctors away.

Bryony and Judy had had few opportunities to talk to each other during the week, their duties not coinciding. On Friday, however, they were both off early and decided to spoil themselves by eating out instead of cooking at the flat.

Seated in Carlo's, their favourite moderately-priced café, they looked forward to catching up on each other's news.

'We'll have your "steak pie like mother makes" please,' Bryony told the dark-jowled little Italian who beamed attendance on them, 'and just an expresso afterwards.'

'John's taking me up to Lincoln to meet his parents as soon as we can fix a weekend together,' confided Judy. 'You do like him, don't you?' she asked, anxious for her friend's approval.

'Of course I do. John's a super guy. Consider yourself lucky if you think you've found your soul mate,' returned Bryony wistfully.

'So what about you and Mike? Anything developing there?'

Bryony shook her head and laughed. 'Heavens, no. We'll never be anything more than mates. Suits me, though. It's rather like having a handy brother. I've always envied people with brothers.' She tackled the piping hot meal which Carlo put before them. 'Mike said he'd come round this evening with some records, in case there's anything we can use for the party.'

'So's John,' said Judy, 'although he may be late since he's on call.' She concentrated on her meal. 'This is good isn't it? Your anorexic could do with a few platefuls of this. Did you get her back, by the way?'

'Sadly, no. Grant Stirling was chocker. Of course it would have to happen on *my* ward, wouldn't it?' Bryony sighed. 'The problems I have with that man.'

Judy raised her eyebrows. 'What is it between you two? A smile from him has most people eating out of his hand.'

'He doesn't happen to favour me with too many of his smiles,' returned Bryony.

Carlo cleared their plates and brought the coffee. Both girls stirred contemplatively.

Glancing absently towards the street door,

Judy's eyes grew suddenly alert. 'Bry . . . don't look now, but you-know-who we were talking about, I think she's just coming in! To your left, with a guy.'

Out of the corner of her eye Bryony stole a glance in the direction indicated. She caught sight of a waif-like girl, shivering in spite of the anorak she was wearing over her jeans. 'You're right,' she murmured, 'it *is* Tina. My God! She looks awful. What do we do now, Judy?'

'A bit of a poser, that,' her friend said, thoughtfully.

It being early evening there was only one other couple in the café besides themselves and the newcomers, but since the nurses were in mufti they were not conspicuous.

'She hasn't noticed us,' Judy went on. Facing the couple, she was more easily able to observe them. 'The boy looks rather nice . . . college scarf . . . older then her by quite a bit, I would think. Looks worried, though. Seems like he's pressuring her to have some soup.'

And then it all started happening. Tina appeared to crumple up. She slithered off her chair to a heap on the floor.

Judy half-rose to her feet. 'Oh help! She's gone out like a light!'

Instantly Bryony pushed back her chair to go to the aid of her ex-patient.

'It's all right, we're nurses and we know Tina,' Judy explained to the alarmed young man while Bryony, on her knees beside the prostrate girl, sat her up and tried to push her head between her knees.

Carlo ran for a glass of water and hovered excitedly, but it soon became clear to the girls that this was no ordinary fainting fit.

Feeling for the pulse, Bryony made an anxious face. Judy raised one of Tina's eyelids and looked at Bryony. 'Do you know what she's been taking?' she asked the concerned young man squatting beside them.

He hesitated. 'We-ell . . . she did say she'd taken some tablets and that they hadn't worked. I-I imagined she meant just a couple, for a headache or something . . .'

'What kind of tablets?' Judy demanded.

'Some of her mother's phenobarb, I think.'

Tina was barely conscious, groaning quietly, her skin clammy and beads of sweat standing out on her lip.

The nurses exchanged worried glances.

'I think we'd better get her to Casualty,' Judy decided for them both. 'Where's your phone, Carlo?'

'This way!' He hurried to show her through to his cluttered office, where she dialled for an ambulance and afterwards alerted the sister in the Casualty Department.

The café was not far from the hospital and during the short time it took for the ambulance to arrive, the boy talked about what had happened.

'I'm a college mate of her brother's, you see. We're at the London together. He'd asked me to pick up his soccer boots since I was popping home for my own gear. When I went round to their house I found Tina all alone there and looking like death warmed up.'

He passed a hand over his troubled face. 'I was amazed to see how thin she'd got . . . she used to be such a jolly kid. She told me her mother was away. I thought she seemed scared, perhaps of being in the house alone, so I suggested taking her out for a meal. That's when she told me she'd taken these tablets. You think she meant an overdose?' He shook his head in disbelief. 'I never dreamed . . .'

Supporting the girl and smoothing the hair from her chalk-white face, Bryony explained: 'Tina's very sick, and she discharged herself from hospital recently.'

The ambulance klaxon could be heard approaching. 'Ah, here it comes,' the boy said with relief. 'I'll go with her, shall I?'

Bryony nodded. 'Yes, if you will. She obviously trusts you, and she needs a friend.'

Back at their flat that evening, with Mike's help the girls had already chosen most of the music for the party before John put in an appearance.

'Hey!' he said with his arms around Judy and pressing his nose to hers, 'You don't have to go out touting for customers for me. I'd have been here much earlier if it hadn't been for Tina Vincent.'

'How is she?' both girls asked.

'Oh, she's back on Addison now. She was okay

after a stomach washout and some i.v. glucose.'
John flopped on the sofa while Judy went to get him
a sandwich and a drink.

'Does Stirling know?' Bryony asked.

'No, he wasn't about. He was changing flats this
evening I believe.'

Mike suddenly jumped up. 'Let's leave these two
to finish up here. Come back to my place for
half-an-hour, Bryony. There's a coupe of buttons I
need altered on my outfit for tomorrow.'

'Why, what are you going to be?' She grabbed
her jacket from the hall as they left the house.

'A pupil nurse. One of the girls lent me a uniform. It's only the belt needs making larger. I
could've used a safety pin, but I thought John
would appreciate us pushing off. They seem to have
clicked, those two.'

'With a little help from my friends!' murmured
Bryony, grinning.

Mike had his rooms in a block of service flats a
short ride away. Leaving his Spitfire parked in the
circular drive, he led Bryony towards the lifts,
saying there was a button needed on one of his
shirts as well, while she was there.

'Why is it I always remind you of running re-
pairs?' she demanded.

He leaned against the lift button, a roguish glint
in his eyes. 'I dunno. Maybe it's because you're
dependable. Your stitching stays put.'

The lift was already on its way down and when
the doors opened, out stepped Grant Stirling with
Vivien.

'Hi!' exclaimed Mike in surprise. 'What are you two doing here?'

'I've just moved into a flat on the fifth floor,' Grant said.

'And I've been helping him,' added Vivien.

'I thought that was your car I saw outside,' Mike went on. 'I live on the third. Come back and have a drink with us?'

Bryony had said nothing at all except a quiet hallo to Vivien. Now she chewed her lip and was heartily glad when Grant declined the invitation.

'Thanks, but not now. Some other time perhaps.'

The couple went on their way while Mike and Bryony stepped into the lift. 'You had a lot to say for yourself just now. Why didn't you help me persuade them?' Mike grumbled.

She tossed her head. 'I prefer not to frat with him.'

'Why not? He's not a bad guy.'

'Oh, we've had one or two differences of opinion.'

Mike threw her a curious glance. 'Not like you . . . what about?'

'This and that.'

'Someone found a chink in your armour, eh?' He laughed and ruffled her hair. 'Ah well, we all have one.'

Arriving at his flat he poured drinks and put on a cassette before finding the button for her to sew on his shirt.

She then stood up to measure the belt of the

uniform around his waist and he pulled her close, smiling into her eyes. 'You're a good kid, Bryony. Don't know why I don't settle for you after all.'

Somehow that evening she couldn't go along with Mike's tomfoolery. 'Oh, pack it up,' she said a little testily. 'I have a say in things too, you know. Let me go, or I'll stick the pin in you.'

He grinned and kissed her before doing as she asked. 'The night is young.'

'No it isn't, and I have to get up in the morning, so I'll just finish this and you can take me back.'

'Bet Vivien wouldn't say that to a chap,' he grumbled.

'Who the hell cares what Vivien does or says?' She pricked her finger on the needle finishing off the belt. 'There you are, you've got blood with it as well,' she said with a wry grin, throwing it at him.

Going on duty the following morning Bryony found Tina back in High Dependancy as John had said. After receiving the night report she went along to have a talk with the teenager.

'I don't know what came over me,' the girl said in a repentant frame of mind and obviously harbouring feelings of guilt about her attempted suicide. 'I was so miserable, I just did it on the spur of the moment. And then, when Dave came round he was so nice to me, I thought what a bother I was being to everyone . . .' The tears welled up into her large brown eyes.

Bryony patted her hand. 'Well, you put all that

behind you now, love. We're going to concentrate on getting you really fit. It won't be easy, but trust us and we'll have you walking out of here looking like a human being in no time.'

Smiling as she spoke, Bryony went on, 'Weren't you lucky your brother's friend called on you? He seems a nice person.'

Tina nodded. 'Dave and my brother were at school together. He was round at our place quite a lot before they started at university.'

'Well, he's already phoned this morning, as well as your brother, to see how you are. Maybe you should write him a thank-you note, when you feel stronger.'

Carrying on with her tour of the patients Bryony felt quite cheered. With Tina's change of attitude her prospects were more hopeful. There would be further setbacks undoubtedly, but even the interest of a young man might help to tip the scales in favour of a complete recovery.

She felt even more cheered that afternoon to have a word of appreciation from Grant Stirling when he came to see the girl.

'I believe we have to thank you and Judy Perrin for a timely rescue operation?' he observed.

'We just happened to be in the right place at the right time,' she replied with a deep sense of satisfaction.

'And so the honour of Addison Ward has been redeemed!' she told Judy blithely as they dressed for their party that night. Fixing her large hoop ear-rings in place and tying the coin-trimmed kerchief over her hair, she studied herself in the mirror. 'I think that'll do me.'

Wriggling into her black leotard, Judy said: 'I'll have to get you to pin my tail on when we get there. It might not be too comfortable to sit on in the car.'

In the doctors' messroom a fair sprinkling of parsons, policemen and pierrots soon appeared among the menfolk, and peasants, princesses and patients among the girls. As Judy had thought, making it a 'P' party added a novel note to their Hallowe'en festivities and the evening went with a swing. Mike Tavistock in his pupil-nurse outfit sported an outstanding bustline and John Dawson was suitably abandoned as a St Trinian's pupil.

Flitting around in her full-skirted gypsy get-up, Bryony gave many palm readings and made some outrageous forecasts. It was their best party ever, she concluded, throwing herself wholeheartedly into the dancing.

That was, until she experienced that uncanny feeling of being under observation again. And when she turned to look, her eyes met the saturnine gaze of the person she knew it would be. Grant Stirling lounged against the bar, glass in hand, his eyes focussed in her direction.

Dancing with all the more abandon she deliberately flirted with Mike, although she couldn't have said what she was trying to prove.

The tape ran out and everyone paused for refreshment. Bryony decided on attack as being the best form of defence. Going up to the bar she challenged the lounge-suited Stirling for not wearing fancy dress.

'And where's your costume?' she asked jauntily.

'I'm a physician, aren't I?' he countered. 'That does begin with a "P".'

She had the grace to laugh. 'That's cheating.'

He looked her over. 'Gypsy doesn't begin with a "P" either.'

'I'm a palmist, of course. Would you like me to read yours?'

'No, let me do the honours.' Putting down his glass he took possession of her hand and began to study it. 'Is this what you call the heart-line?' He traced the crease in her palm with a long, firm finger. 'Trouble ahead there, I can see. Beware of a false friend!'

She knew he was getting at Mike and attempted to pull her hand away in annoyance. He held on tightly and continued to examine her palm with pretended expertise. 'Hm . . . a strong lifeline . . . you should live to a ripe old age.'

'You won't, if you don't watch it!' she warned.

He proceeded to count the creases beneath her little finger. 'One, two, three children.'

'Have you finished?'

'Not yet.' The corners of his mouth twitched. 'Now we come to character. Capable, but given to self-doubt. A good friend, but a bad enemy.' He shook his head in mock reproof. 'Loyal, but apt to be taken advantage of . . .'

Again she tried to put a stop to the proceedings.

'Oh, come on, joke over,' she said with an embarrassed laugh.

But he had not finished with her. 'Keep still! You're spoiling my vibrations. I foresee you making a long journey soon . . .'

'You don't read that kind of thing in a palm,' she snapped.

'Ah, but I'm psychic as well. There's another "P" for you. It'll be a road journey . . . in the company of someone you don't much care for . . . I get the impression. Would you care to know his name?'

She looked into his bland face with a startled air. She had a suspicion he might not now be playacting.

'Haven't you had a letter?' he enquired.

'I get lots of letters. Who's this supposed to be from?'

He raised an eyebrow equivocally. 'Since you appear to be in the dark, let me tell you a story. Once upon a time there were two schoolboys. When they grew up one of them went to Australia, and he had a son. The other stayed in England, and he had a daughter. And the son, who studied medicine, came back to England.'

The truth slowly began to dawn on Bryony. She caught her breath. 'Oh no! It's not *you*?'

Grant Stirling laughed softly. 'I'm afraid so. Small world. But I thought you didn't know anything about it?'

She drew another deep breath and wished the floor would swallow her up. 'I-I . . . my mother phoned while I was out. She did tell Judy a bit of the story, but she didn't mention you by name, or that you were at the Heathside.'

'I see. I thought perhaps that you . . . well, never mind. Your father told me you were planning a visit home next weekend and he invited me along. We may as well travel together,' he went on briskly. 'I shall need a navigator, I haven't been to the west country before. Good! I'm glad we've got that sorted out.' He finished his drink. 'I'll let you know details later,' and he calmly took himself off, leaving her exasperated to the point of tears.

The cheek of the man! she fumed. How dare he assume that she would simply go along with whatever plans he cared to make?

Judy was no consolation. On learning what had transpired she roared with laughter. 'Now you'll have to be nice to him,' she said. It ruined the end of the party for Bryony.

Early on Sunday morning she seized the opportunity to phone home.

'Oh, so you've heard from Dr Stirling already then?' her mother answered brightly. 'Sorry you didn't get my letter first . . . it's in the post now. Dad was selling some stock over at Bampton and I went with him, which was what held me up.'

'So fill me in,' said Bryony, stifling a groan. 'I wish you'd told Judy who he was and that he worked at the Heathside.'

'We didn't actually know that until he phoned in answer to Dad's letter. You see, your dad and his were in the Navy together after they left school. 'Then Chas Stirling emigrated to Australia.

They've kept in touch over the years, and when he wrote to Dad saying his son was over here, naturally your father thought it would be a nice gesture to meet the boy,' Mrs Clemence explained. 'The address we had was one in Scotland, but Dad's letter was forwarded on, and that's the whole story.'

'But, about us travelling down together, I mean who suggested that?'

'I don't know,' her mother said, 'he was talking to Dad at the time. It probably seemed the most sensible arrangement. Rather sweet of him, I thought, agreeing to make it the same weekend as you if he possibly could. If he drives you down it'll save us the trip to Exeter. What's he like?' Mrs Clemence wanted to know. 'He sounded an agreeable young fellow. Dad says Chas Stirling was an easy-going sort of chap . . . probably takes after him.'

Sweet? Agreeable? Easy-going? They were the last qualities Bryony would have ascribed to Grant Stirling. She could think of nothing worse than a five-hour drive in his company, plus a whole weekend of having to be charming to him.

At home she always looked forward to relaxing, messing about in comfortable old clothes with her hair blowing free as she walked with the dogs on the moors. But this time, with everything having been decided over her head it would be a far from carefree break. It would be like treading a tight-rope, trying to keep the peace with him.

With a sigh of resignation Bryony supposed she

had better grin and bear it. After all, it was most likely to be a once only occasion; for her parents' sake at least she ought to put on a show of being sociable.

'I suppose you would call him good-looking,' she allowed, 'but apart from coming in contact with him on the ward, I really don't know him very well.'

'That should give you a nice lot to talk about on the way down,' her mother enthused. 'And there's lots of things we can show him once you're here, so keep your fingers crossed for good weather.'

Bryony had to console herself with the thought that the return journey would be made on her own. For her few days extra leave after the weekend she would be free of him.

# CHAPTER FIVE

ALTHOUGH Bryony saw Grant a good deal during the course of her work the following week, their talk was confined to ward matters. About the proposed visit to her parents' farm nothing more was said. Perhaps he was not able to get away, she speculated hopefully. Or her own leave might have to be postponed with Sister McCullagh off sick.

By mid-week, however, the senior sister was back at work, although still blowing her nose frequently. 'Didn't want to risk messing up your leave,' she said nobly, 'I know how much you've been looking forward to it.' •

While being duly appreciative Bryony privately fell back on the possibility that Grant's arrangements would go adrift. But no such miracle occurred.

At the close of his ward round on Friday afternoon he came back to the office to speak to her.

'How soon can you be ready, Bryony? What time shall I pick you up . . . five . . . five-thirty?'

'Oh! It's still on then, your weekend?' she queried.

'Of course. I can leave any time now.' He glanced at her keenly. 'You're not too enthusiastic about the arrangement?'

It occurred to her that she was being a little ungracious, letting her reluctance show through when he was probably merely trying to be accommodating. She smiled and apologised, 'Sorry, I didn't intend it to sound like that. You know how it is with you doctors, you can never be sure of getting away until you're actually on the road.'

Coming in and overhearing bits of the conversation Sister McCullagh looked intrigued. 'Oh, you can push off a bit early, Bryony. Goodness knows, you've put in enough extra time lately one way and another.'

And so by five o'clock Grant was outside Bryony's flat, loading her sizeable suitcase into the boot of his silver Talbot.

He remarked at the weight of it. 'Ye gods! You certainly don't believe in travelling light. Sorry!' He held up a placatory hand as she opened her mouth to protest, 'I remember . . . you're staying on after the weekend, aren't you?' His voice took on a bantering note. 'So if my presence proves to be a trial to you, you'll be able to make up for it when I've gone.'

Determined to keep the peace, she gave him a honeyed smile. 'There's no reason why it should be. *I* shall be on my best behaviour, I can assure you.' Taking her seat beside him she went on: 'I can't imagine what Sister McCullagh will make of this. She was looking distinctly coy when I left.'

'Women!' drawled Grant, starting up the engine, 'The female mind is always match-making.'

She hooted at that. 'A typically male viewpoint.

Anyway, you need have no worries on my score.'

It was already dusk with a faint mist falling as they drove out of London through the home-going traffic. By the time they reached the open road the rain had begun to fall in earnest. But the atmosphere inside the car was, surprisingly enough, cheerful. There was pleasant music from the radio to break their silences. She was looking forward to going home, and he was apparently trying to be amenable.

'It's a pity you'll be seeing Exmoor for the first time this late in the year,' she chatted. 'Of course, there's the heather, and the autumn colours, but in the spring it's really gorgeous.'

'My father always told me it was a wild sort of place,' Grant said, 'but I expect it's changed a lot since he was there.'

'Oh, it's still pretty wild in parts, especially now with the rivers getting swollen. We do have rather a lot of rain down there.'

'Yes, my father remembered that too. And he told me about the times they were snowed in and couldn't get to school.'

'When did he go to Australia? Did he marry out there?'

Grant's relaxed expression tightened. He shook his head, replying tersely, 'I was four before my parents emigrated. I don't remember much about it. He's still in sheep, like your father . . . he still says there's nothing to beat the horned Exmoor breed. But I guess he's happy enough with his present way of life.'

Before she could ask more questions he went on: 'Tell me about your folks.'

Bryony dragged her eyes from the contemplation of his firm chin-line. 'Well, we live in a very old farmhouse in a village on the edge of Exmoor; my grandparents had it before us. Mostly it's sheep, but Dad grows a few crops, and there's a cider-apple orchard. My mother keeps free-range hens and looks after baby lambs when they need looking after. Then there's my young sister, Joanne, who's potty about music and ponies. A cat, and two dogs, and me, and that's it. My mother was a nurse, too,' she went on to say. 'She's always telling me how much better things are these days than when she was training.'

He gave a twisted smile. 'Mmm, that's true in some ways, but the march of time doesn't always change things for the better.'

She was left wondering if the remark had any special significance for him, but she didn't comment.

Her eyes moved to the windscreen where the wipers moved rhythmically back and forth, clearing away the muddy spray flung up from passing traffic. Their headlights lit up the wet road, contrasting with the comfort of the warmth inside the car.

Having left the confines of the hospital with its disciplined atmosphere, their relationship did seem less fraught, she mused. They were simply a man and a girl making a journey together and passing the time in light conversation.

She had ample opportunity for observing him

during the journey. Now and again he would glance briefly in her direction or smile disarmingly at some remark of hers.

She found herself following the movement of his shapely mouth when he spoke, liking the way his teeth were not quite regular in front, and the way his rich brown hair fell across his forehead. His deep and vibrant voice had a subtle magnetism that she found fascinating.

It was a little while before Bryony could force herself to face the truth. She had to admit that against all her inclinations she was powerfully attracted by this man. Even that cool, detached smile of his made her bones feel weak. Which was a ridiculous state of affairs when she didn't even like him very much. Didn't *want* to like him since he was completely indifferent to her.

Besides which, there was Vivien. Other people had seen them together on a number of occasions and in Bryony's book one certainly did not go breaking up someone else's romance, especially someone as nice as Vivien. She decided she had better keep a tight rein on this purely physical pull he seemed to be exerting over her.

They had been on the road for a good three hours now, with the weather getting steadily worse. There was no opportunity to admire picturesque Somerset towns and quaint villages in the rain-washed landscape. The folding hills were mysterious mounds of darkness.

Coming to a signpost on the Devon borders, she pointed him in the right direction. He had to put total concentration into driving, peering ahead with the windscreen wipers working at double speed. The downpour had increased to such intensity that the road was like a river. Water cascaded down the car windows with each renewed burst of fury. It became impossible to go on.

Slowing to a crawl, Grant drew into the shelter of a large tree by the side of the desolate road. He switched off the engine and stretched out with his hands behind his head.

'When it rains here, it certainly rains!' he said lazily. 'When this eases off a bit perhaps we should find somewhere to eat. You could ring your folks and explain that we may be a little late, hm?'

His eyes met hers, and again she felt that unwelcome tingle down her spine.

Before she could answer a violent gust of wind flung an even greater deluge at the car. Lightning lit the sky. Thunder crackled immediately overhead.

Bryony started. He put an arm along the back of her seat. 'Scared?'

She gave a shaky laugh. 'No! It was a bit unexpected, that's all.'

Another vivid blue flash broke the darkness, followed at once by another ear-splitting rumble. She resisted the temptation to bury her face on his shoulder and sat up determinedly.

Anxious to be out of this all-too-intimate situation she shaded her eyes to scan their whereabouts.

'I think I can see a pub sign just along the road,' she said. 'If you can make it as far as that we might just as well be eating as sitting here. They'll probably be able to find us some sandwiches if nothing else.'

'Good thinking,' agreed Grant. He started up the car and crept the short distance to the gravelled car park by the side of the Leaping Stag, a grey-stoned hostelry whose lights winked invitingly.

'Going to make a dash for it?' Grant reached onto the back seat for his leather jacket as another outburst of thunder rolled around. 'You're going to get wet!'

'I'll be okay.' Bryony slipped the hood of her quilted raincoat over her head, opened the car door and ran. It was only a few yards to the inn entrance, but even so her shoes were squelching and her face dripping water as, breathless and laughing, she held open the door for Grant who came sprinting after her.

Pushing through an inner door, they found themselves in a warm saloon bar with a low black-raftered ceiling and a crackling log fire at one end.

Bryony went to the open hearth to warm herself, taking off her coat and shaking drops off the ends of her hair.

The side-whiskered landlord behind the cluttered bar hailed them warmly as he rinsed some tankards. 'Good evening! *Not* a very good one, though, I'm afraid.'

'You can say that again!' Grant stamped his feet and squeezed the water from his hair.

A couple of local old-timers, sitting at an oak settle with their pints, gazed at the newcomers with mild interest.

The landlord passed Grant a paper towel to mop his face and said to Bryony: 'I should go to the cloakroom, m'dear. You'll find a towel in there.'

'Thanks, I will.' She disappeared to tidy up.

Upon her return Grant was deep in conversation at the bar. He paused to call, 'What will you have?'

'A dry sherry, please.' She seated herself at the table nearest the fire and stretched out her legs to dry.

He brought the drink over to her together with his own. 'Soup and grilled plaice coming up soon. How does that grab you?'

'Lovely,' Bryony said.

'They say we won't get much further tonight. It's been raining like this for twenty-four hours. Roads flooded, detours everywhere.' Grant's brow creased. 'Bit of a problem, isn't it?'

'Where be you making for exactly?' one of the locals piped up.

'South Molton way,' Bryony said.

All the company shook their heads and made sceptical noises. They were unanimous in their opinion that it would be madness to attempt the journey that night.

Grant turned to the landlord. 'Could you help us out? Do you have accommodation?'

'Oh, aye. There's a couple of rooms for visitors, but that's the wife's side of things. I'll have a word with her. I expect she can fix you up.'

'I'd better phone home right away then,' Bryony said to Grant, and she went to the public telephone in the vestibule.

There was considerable relief in her father's voice when she managed to get through. 'We were beginning to get worried about you, there are so many trees down, and landslips. Yes, it'll be much wiser for you to come on in the morning, especially since Dr Stirling isn't familiar with our country roads. See you sometime tomorrow then, love.'

'Get through all right?' Grant asked pleasantly when she went back to join him at the table by the fire.

'Oh yes, and they agree it'll be better for us to come on in the morning.'

She felt somewhat nervous. The weekend was not working out quite as planned. Once the journey was over she had thought to hand Grant over to the family to entertain. She hadn't anticipated a solitary evening spent in his company. After they had eaten, she wondered, would it seem odd if she took herself off to her room? With her legs and feet still wet from the storm she could make the excuse of needing to get out of her damp clothes. Grant could chat on with the men in the bar if he wished.

The landlord's wife brought in their soup and assured them that she could fix them up for the night.

Satisfied, Grant tucked into his bowl of country broth with relish.

It was a sizeable helping and Bryony could only manage half of hers.

There followed a generous portion of fish topped with a creamy sauce.

'Bon appetit!' Grant raised his glass to hers

before starting his meal. 'I'm certainly ready for this.'

Very much on edge, Bryony had no appetite.

The firelight played across Grant's strong features, lighting his clear, keen eyes. 'Is anything the matter?' he asked as she laid down her knife and fork. 'I mean, apart from our interrupted journey?'

It was almost as though he were hyper-sensitive to her mounting tension. She made an effort to sound casual. 'No, I'm just not very hungry.'

'Well, you should be. You haven't eaten for . . .' he glanced towards the ancient grandfather clock ticking away in a corner of the saloon, 'what is it . . . nine hours?'

She made a show of smothering a yawn. 'The soup was filling, and I'm tired. All I really want to do is to get out of these damp things and go to bed.'

'Okay, we'll call it a day. I can do with some shut-eye myself. I'll get your bag for you.'

'Bad as ever out there, sir,' the landlord put in. 'Throw this over your head,' and he produced a yellow waterproof cape from a peg behind the counter.

Suitably protected, Grant braved the elements, returning in a few moments with their luggage and leaving a trail of drips in his wake.

'You were right!' he laughed, returning the waterproof, 'It doesn't show any signs of letting up yet.'

'Want to go upstairs now, do you? Right, I'll call the missus,' the landlord said. 'She'll probably find

you a hot-water bottle if you want it. You'll soon
get nice and snug.' Summoning his wife to show
them the way, he bade them goodnight.

They followed the good lady up a narrow, un-
even flight of creaking stairs, down a sloping passage and up another small flight. Reaching the
landing, she opened the door of a dormer room
with its floor at as crazy an angle as its ceiling. But it
was nicely decorated and quite sizeable.

'There you are, my dears,' she said with some
pride. 'That's a new mattress on the bed, and the
bathroom's just across the landing. We only have
the two rooms – this and one on the floor below, but
a commercial gent's got that. You're lucky this one
happened to be free. What time will you be wanting
breakfast, sir?'

'Oh, er, I should think about eight, wouldn't
you, Bryony?' Grant nudged her.

Bryony's saucer eyes were fixed on the double
bed in the centre of the room. She gulped and
swallowed. 'Oh, er, yes . . . fine!'

'Goodnight, then. Sleep well.' The landlady
beamed at them and went out, closing the door
quietly behind her.

Spinning round, Bryony faced the now grinning
Grant. 'Well!' she flared, 'I did wonder if we might
have to share a room, but I'm damned if I'm going
to share your bed!'

He passed a hand over his mouth in an effort to
control his amusement. 'I'm afraid you've no op-
tion . . . unless you prefer to sleep on the floor. I
certainly don't intend to.'

She glowered at him. 'No Sir Galahad, are you? Did you know it was a double?'

'Honestly, it didn't occur to me that it would be. In any case it's the only room available, so you'll have to put up with it.'

His arrogance was infuriating. She glanced wildly around the room. There was not even an easy chair, just a pair of white-painted chairs on either side of a small table.

'Oh, grow up, girl,' he scoffed. 'You can stuff a pillow between us if you're scared of me. But I wouldn't touch you with a barge pole . . . I only bed willing partners.'

Flinging him a withering glance she opened her suitcase, rummaged for nightdress, dressing-gown and toilet bag and stormed past him to the bathroom.

The water was moderately hot, she found. But although a warm soak was comforting to her chilled feet it did little to allay the panic inside her. She was going to have to spend the night sharing a bed with this man. How could she bear it when even to be in his company stirred up emotions she hadn't thought possible in herself?

Normally she was a level-headed, responsible twenty-three-year-old, and now she was reacting like an adolescent. This was the way her young sister went on with each new heart-throb. It might be amusing in a schoolgirl, but it was plain idiocy in an adult.

'There's plenty of water,' she told him, distantly, coming back ready for bed and draping her damp clothes over the back of one of the chairs.

'Thank you,' he returned, equally distant. He had already stripped off his shirt. He had a powerful, muscular torso and his shoulder muscles rippled as he slung pyjama trousers over his arm and disappeared, barefoot, towards the bathroom.

While he was gone she did consider folding back the bedclothes to make two separate halves. But he would be bound to make some caustic comment if she did that. Quickly she jumped into bed pulling her pillows away from his and keeping as far to one side as possible.

Again telling herself how stupid it was to be physically drawn to someone you didn't even like, she nevertheless pondered how romantic the situation could have been, if things were different.

The room itself had an old-world charm despite some twentieth-century improvements. There were chintzy curtains at the casement windows and an oatmeal shagpile carpet on the floor. Oak beams seamed the plain magnolia walls and the wardrobe and dressing-table belonged to Victoriana. A modern central-heating radiator took the chill off the room and a pink-shaded bedside lamp cast its pattern across the sloping white ceiling.

Glancing upwards, Bryony suddenly froze with horror. Dangling over her head on a flimsy thread was the largest, hairiest spider she had ever seen. Busily spinning a web, it swung alarmingly towards the wall.

With a squeak of fright Bryony shot to the other end of the bed just as Grant re-entered in his

pyjama trousers. 'What's wrong now?' he demanded, with an exaggerated show of patience.

She pointed and shuddered. 'C-could you please
do something about that? I-I can't st-stand spiders.'

With a patronising smirk he climbed onto the
bed, gathered the offending creature into his hand
and returned to throw it out of the window.

'There you are, Miss Muffet. I'm surprised at
you, a country girl, being scared of spiders.'

'I don't mind them in their proper place . . . it's
in the house I don't like them.' She scanned the
ceiling timidly and pointed, 'Th-there's another
one up there. Would you . . . ?'

Sighing tolerantly he disposed of a smaller spider
in the same way as the first. 'They've come in out of
the rain, I expect. They're harmless. Now if you
were in Australia you would be right to be scared.
Over there you never put your shoes on without
banging them first, just in case there are any black
widows hiding.' He slid beneath the covers on his
side of the bed. 'You'll get cold if you sit there much
longer with so little on. Put the light out when
you're ready.' Turning on his side, he settled down
to sleep.

Bryony crept back between the covers and
switched off the lamp. She lay as near to the edge of
the bed as possible so that their bodies did not
touch. Since his bulk was greater than hers there
was a draught down the middle. The bed creaked
horribly every time she tried to get comfortable.

Closing her eyes she listened to the steady hiss of
rain on the windows. It was no good . . . she

couldn't settle, still thinking of spiders. After about ten minutes she had to sit up, switch on the light again and search the ceiling above her head.

'Grant!' she said in a small voice.

He didn't bother to move. 'What is it now?'

'I-I'm sorry, Grant. I-I shan't be able to sleep like this. I—could we pull the bed away from the wall a bit . . . just in case . . .'

'My God!' he exclaimed wearily, and leaping up he yanked the bed, with her in it, into the middle of the room. 'There you are. Now, is there anything else? Would you like a bedtime story, perhaps?'

She mustered the shreds of her dignity. 'Thank you. Sorry. But I daresay you have your pet aversions as well.'

'And one of them is little girls who won't let me get my rest!' He tucked her in rather roughly. 'If you get any nearer the edge you'll fall out! Goodnight!'

He switched off the light and she heard him curse beneath his breath as he banged himself finding his way round to his side of the bed.

She lay there feeling shivery.

'Stop rocking the boat!' he muttered.

'Well, I'm cold. I should have asked for that hot-water bottle.'

'Help yourself to my central heating,' came his muffled voice, 'I'm always warm.'

She hesitated before inching her feet over to rest against his warm legs.

'Ouch! They're like blocks of ice!' he growled, and turning over, put his arm across her, pulling her towards him. 'Come on, don't be an idiot. I'm not a rapist and I don't bite, either. The sooner you get warm the sooner we can both get to sleep.'

She lay stiff as a ramrod for a few moments, resisting with all her might the disturbing power of his animal closeness. But it was really very comforting to be cuddled against his warm body. Listening to his quiet breathing she at last relaxed. Sleep overtook her, but it was not a deep, refreshing rest, more a series of dream-filled dozes.

In the bright morning light she awoke heavy-eyed and sat up with a jerk remembering where she was. Had she really passed a night in bed with Grant, falling asleep in his arms? It seemed like a part of her troubled dreams. His side of the bed was now empty, but the sheets were crumpled and there was the distinct imprint of where his head had been upon the pillow. She wondered when they had become disentangled. Half-relieved to find him gone, she yet felt strangely piqued. 'For all the effect I had on you, G.S., I might as well have been a stuffed pillow.'

Slipping into her dressing-gown and gathering up her clothes, she made for the bathroom only to find it locked.

'Five minutes!' came Grant's voice as she tried the handle.

Trailing back to the bedroom she deposited her things on the bed and crossed to look out of the window. The rain had stopped and a watery sun was breaking through, glinting on the bedraggled gardens at the back of the inn.

She was glad at least that bad weather would not keep them tied to the house once they reached her home. The farm was on high ground and in an area not subject to flooding. Her father would most likely have plans to show Grant the neighbourhood, which would keep him usefully entertained until it was time for him to leave.

She did not hear him return from the bathroom until, already dressed, he came up behind her to look over her shoulder. 'Good morning. I trust you slept well in the end?'

Now that the night was safely behind her she felt more able to disregard his lofty overtones. 'Yes, thank you!' she returned levelly in spite of the fluttery feeling in her throat when she turned round to find him studying her. 'Did you?'

'Like a top.'

'Good. Well,' she went on, 'it seems to have cleared up. It shouldn't take us too long to get home now, provided the roads are okay.' Anxious to be away from his penetrating gaze she made to pass him to pick up her things from the bed.

'Just a moment,' he put a hand on her shoulder, 'What's that in your hair?'

Cringing, she let out a squeal of alarm. 'Take it off! Take it off!'

'Calm down, it's only a brown feather out of the pillow.' He picked it out to show her.

She turned on him in fury, hammering at his chest with her fists. 'You beast! You absolute beast! You—you did that on purpose, you sadist.'

'Hold it!' He seized her wrists and forced them

behind her back to stop her onslaught. 'What did you think it was, a spider? My God! You must have a low opinion of me if you think I'd exploit your phobia.'

With bodies touching they stood glaring at each other. She fought to free herself, her emotions in turmoil at their physical contact. Tears started to her eyes. His breath came heavily, hot on her face. And the next moment his mouth found hers in a fierce, demanding kiss.

She was gasping and tremulous when he at last released her. 'You've been asking for that,' was his brusque explanation. 'Either that, or a spanking.'

'A-and you dare to criticise Mike Tavistock for playing the field?' flared Bryony, livid with anger and humiliation. 'What about Vivien?'

His hard expression softened somewhat. 'Ah yes, Vivien. Thanks for reminding me.'

'Oh, you're absolutely odious. I hate you!'

'I'll try to forget you said that,' was his curt rejoinder, 'otherwise it's going to be a difficult weekend. Now off you go and get dressed for breakfast.' He slapped her, not at all gently, on the rear.

Two breakfast trays had been brought to the bedroom by the time she returned. At the small table they sat opposite each other in stony silence, but this time Bryony did full justice to the meal of egg and bacon, hot rolls and coffee.

'I'm glad you've found your appetite,' said Grant.

She did not deign to reply.

'How long are you proposing to keep up this cold war?'

She made herself meet his accusing eyes. 'You behaved abominably.'

'No-one shows their claws to me and gets away with it.'

She drank some coffee to give herself time to gain control. 'For my parents' sake, and only that, I am prepared to bury the hatchet for the time being.'

'Thank you.' There was something suspiciously like laughter in his voice. 'Is it pax, then?' He held out his little finger for her to latch on to, an impudent gleam in the depths of his grey-green eyes.

'Don't be childish,' she murmured.

'When you behave childishly what else can you expect?'

She resisted the desire to throw something at him. 'We'd better be on our way before my folks send out a search party,' she said, on her dignity.

# CHAPTER SIX

THE sun had come out in earnest as Bryony and Grant took their leave of the innkeeper and his wife. With many warnings to look out for mud on the roads, they set off on the last stage of their journey.

A guarded truce prevailed. Bryony, having decided that a polite indifference was the best approach, limited her initial remarks to comments on the storm damage. Where the road undulated they passed many fields still waterlogged, and everywhere there were boughs torn from trees and debris littering the ground. But at least the brighter weather showed the landscape to good advantage. Many trees had still to shed their leaves and sunlight burnishing autumn tints lifted her spirits as the car ate up the miles towards her home.

'I hadn't realised how homesick I was,' she admitted, 'and yet it's only three months since I was there. Do you get homesick for Australia?'

'I miss the sunshine, of course,' Grant answered, 'but I'm a self-sufficient sort of guy. I've been a kind of nomad, I suppose you could say, for the last twelve years. Medical school in Sydney; various other places since. I haven't spent a great deal of time back home.'

'That must be tough on your folks,' Bryony said.

'My mother would be heart-sick if she couldn't keep tabs on her family.'

'Oh, my mother walked out on Dad and me when I was ten years old.' Grant slowed the car as they squelched through a deep puddle in the road, sending a spray of rusty water flying.

She stole a rapid glance at his face, feeling a wave of pity for an abandoned child as she pictured the desertion. But his expression was quite bland as he changed gear to gather speed.

'Did your father marry again?' she prompted, trying not to sound too curious.

'No. Once was enough.' There was a satirical twist to Grant's mouth. 'The sheep station occupies all his time. But we were good pals, the two of us.'

'Didn't your mother keep in touch with you?' she was moved to ask.

'Oh yes. She had me for the holidays. That's how I came to spend some time over here. It didn't work out all that well. Probably my fault; I couldn't forgive her. Children don't make allowances for human failings.'

Bryony was thoughtful. 'No, things are either right or wrong to children. No grey areas. Do you see her now?'

He shook his head, looking regretful. 'She died rather tragically when I was in my teens; she and the man she married. It was a faulty gas-fire in a caravan. I thought it was poetic justice, but my father wept.'

'I'm so sorry,' Bryony said.

He shrugged. 'It's strange how life works out.

Destiny or design, it caused me to meet someone who became a major influence in my life. If it hadn't been for that I might not be here now.' He didn't explain further and she presumed he must be referring to Vivien.

'You should have told my folks about Vivien,' she said. 'I'm sure they would have included her in their invitation.'

Halting at a 'T' junction, he flung her a mystified glance. 'You do have a grasshopper mind. In any case, Vivien's in study block at the moment. Which way now?'

She looked to the great expanse of the moor rolling ahead with its distant purple hills and browning bracken and hummocky grass. 'Um, right, I should think. Although I wonder if we could risk it across the moor?'

'Why, what's the risk?'

'Nothing really. By daylight it's not a bad road. Providing we don't run out of petrol or break down, it would be quicker. But it's fifteen miles of ups and downs and not a sign of habitation.'

His mouth twitched. 'Do I take it I'm back in favour since you're prepared even to consider it?'

'I'd just prefer to end this *tête-á-tête* as soon as possible,' she retorted.

He took the lonely moorland road. 'We shan't get stranded, I can promise you. I always carry a can of gas in the boot.'

'Nothing catches you out, does it?' There was a hint of sarcasm in her voice.

'Not if I can help it.'

Through the rolling moorland cloud shadows played over the sunlit hills and nothing disturbed the peace save the cry of curlews. The only other life they met was a bunch of Exmoor ponies which galloped away, manes flying, at the approach of the car.

Within forty minutes they had reached the outskirts of the remote village and the high-banked lane leading to Clemence Farm.

As the car crunched to a halt outside the double gates leading to the drive, the dogs started barking. Despite the lateness of the season there were still flowers blooming around the perimeter of the whitewashed farmhouse, Bryony noticed with pleasure, jumping out of the car to open the gates for Grant.

Mrs Clemence appeared in the doorway of the house, a welcoming smile on her face.

'Hi, Mum!' Bryony waved, pausing to shut the gates again after the car had gone through, before running to be hugged and to fondle the two dogs who came to add their welcome. 'Hallo, you two!' She stooped to scratch their ears.

'We were glad you found somewhere to stay last night. What a storm, wasn't it?' her mother said. 'And this must be Dr Stirling.' Mrs Clemence went forward, extending her hand to Grant who had alighted and leaned against the car bonnet, waiting.

Bryony remembered her manners. 'Oh, sorry, Grant. This is my mother. And here's Dad.' She went to meet the burly tweed-suited figure, trousers tucked into gumboots, who came striding around the corner.

'So here you are at last!' Farmer Clemence embraced his daughter and shook hands with their visitor. 'And I don't need any introduction to you, young man.' He turned to his wife. 'Did you ever see anyone so like his father?'

'I don't know dear. I've only seen your faded old snapshots.' Mrs Clemence chuckled and looked up into Grant's good-humoured face. 'You're going to be heartily sick of old photographs and reminiscing by the time you go back to London. My husband's been looking them out all week.'

She led the way into the living-room, inviting him to a seat on the chintz-covered sofa. 'Do sit down. How long can you stay with us?'

'I shall have to leave tomorrow evening, if that's convenient for you, Mrs Clemence.'

'Oh, what a shame to come all this way for such a short visit. That doesn't mean you too, Bryony?' her mother asked.

'No, you've got me till Friday. Aren't you lucky?' Bryony grinned, tickling the tummy of Lady, the older dog who fawned at her feet. 'Where's Joanne?'

'At her music lesson, but she shouldn't be long now. I expect you can both do with a drink; I'll get some coffee.'

Bryony followed her mother into the kitchen to talk while her father sat down with Grant to catch up on news of his old friend in Australia.

'Yes, I reckon we've done pretty well to keep our

correspondence going all these years,' Bryony heard her father saying as she carried in the tray of coffee and her mother's home-baked shortbread. 'I keep telling him it's about time he paid the old country a visit.'

'Well, you know what it's like, farms are difficult to leave,' said Grant, 'but maybe he'll get around to it one of these days.'

A tinkling bicycle bell outside signalled the arrival home of Bryony's young sister.

'Here comes trouble!' breezed their father as the rosy-cheeked sixteen-year-old came bounding in, eager-eyed and curious, to be introduced.

'And what are your plans for the future?' Grant asked the youngster as they lingered over coffee. 'Are you set on following in the footsteps of your mother and sister?'

'Be a nurse, you mean? Heavens, no.' Joanne shuddered. 'Blood anywhere but in its proper channels scares me stiff.'

'Ah well, everyone's scared of something.' Grant darted a meaningful glance in Bryony's direction. 'So what *are* you going to do with your life?'

'Get married and have babies.'

'So long as it's in that order I shan't complain,' said her father amid general laughter.

There followed a discussion of proposed plans for the weekend before Grant went out to fetch the luggage from the car prior to being taken on a tour of inspection of the farm by Mr Clemence.

It left the sisters free to talk while Bryony unpacked in her bedroom.

'He's dishy,' Joanne said approvingly. 'Are you having an affair with him?'

Bryony snorted. 'Don't be silly. If he weren't the son of Dad's old schoolmate we'd only be on nodding terms. And I expect that's the way it will be as soon as we get back to the hospital.'

'But he likes you. I could tell the way he was looking at you,' insisted Joanne.

'You've been reading too many romantic novels,' Bryony laughed. 'Anyway, he's got a girlfriend.'

'Oh, pity.'

'Sorry to disappoint you, but this was purely a journey of convenience.' Bryony changed the subject. 'And how's the love of your life?'

'Tony? Oh, you can meet him tonight at the Young Farmers' Martinmas Social, but I've gone off him, a bit.'

'I thought *this was it*!' teased Bryony.

Joanne wrinkled her pert nose. 'He knows *nothing* about Chopin. You've got to have things in common, haven't you? Isn't it good I'm on half-term while you're here?' She held up a floaty Indian cotton dress of her sister's, measuring it against herself. 'I love this. Pity it's too long for me . . . I could've borrowed it for the social.'

'Tough!' Bryony grinned, hanging it up. 'I shall probably wear it myself in any case.'

Joanne flopped on the bed. 'Will he want to come, do you think?'

'You mean Grant, to the social? I thought we were all going?'

'Mum and Dad didn't know whether it would appeal to him. I mean, he might've been a pain, but he isn't, is he?'

Bryony screwed up her nose. 'Far too sure of himself for my liking.'

'Oh well, I'd better get some practice in before they come back. I've got a new piece by Coleridge-Taylor for my exam.' Joanne skimmed downstairs and presently the sound of her music could be heard.

Following later, Bryony went into the kitchen to see if she could help. Lunch was almost ready, so she went about setting the table in the living-room. Shaking out the clean cloth, she was humming to the hesitant strain of Joanne's 'Demande et Reponse' when the menfolk returned.

Grant sauntered over to the piano, hands in pockets, watching the young player with an air of interest.

'Go away. You're making me nervous,' giggled Joanne, looking up at him shyly. She made to shut the music but Grant prevented her.

'Move over!' he commanded and seating himself on the wide stool to her left, he slipped an arm around her waist. 'You concentrate on the right hand while I play the base.'

Joanne looked at him in pleased surprise. 'Do you play?'

'Get on with it,' he prompted.

Together the two of them made a tuneful noise. It was obvious that besides his other skills Grant was an accomplished musician. At the end of the

piece they congratulated each other with a handshake and changed seats so that she could tackle the
left hand.

'How did you find time to learn the piano as well
as everything else?' Joanne asked.

He winked at her. 'Maybe I had to miss out on a
few things like Young Farmers' socials.'

'Oh, but you don't mind coming tonight?'

'I've only got casual gear with me. Is that
okay?'

Bryony glanced up from putting knives and forks
in place. 'That'll do. It won't be a smart affair like
Sir Phinny's.'

'What was that?' Joanne wanted to know.
Whereupon Grant launched into a graphic account
of the party at Kensington, sending his young
listener into peals of laughter. It was quite obvious
that he had completely charmed the youngest
member of the family.

Bryony couldn't help feeling a twinge of envy at
the ease with which the two of them carried on
chatting as they tried some more music. No friction
there! She remembered the audacity of his far from
fleeting kiss at that party, and the more brutal one
he had pressed on her earlier that day. Thinking
ahead to the evening it was reassuring that she was
bound to know a good number of people. It would
be the usual homely, friendly occasion with novelty
dances and games. With a bit of luck she need not
have to endure too many awkward moments with
Grant to shake her fragile defences.

With lunch over everyone piled into Mr Clemence's estate car for a sight-seeing tour of the haunts of days gone by.

'The place has hardly changed at all since your dad and I were boys,' Bryony's father said, parking in the hilly market town and pointing out the old grammar school where both fathers had been pupils.

Grant found plenty of subjects for his camera. He clicked away, taking pictures of the fifteenth-century church, the old guildhall and magnificent views of rolling hills that could be glimpsed on all sides. 'Dad said he'd like to see if things were still as he remembered them. He'll be disappointed if I don't include a picture of you all.' So saying, he grouped them outside the old thatched tea-rooms and took several shots before they went inside for a cream tea.

That evening, in a church hall in the town, the Martinmas Social proved to be the expected hotch-potch of entertainment that had been traditional ever since Bryony could remember.

Without the usual courtesy of first asking, Grant commandeered her for the first dance. With his arms firmly about her, she tried to steel herself against the spell of his touch. But the material of her dress was thin and the warm vitality of his body against her own aroused emotions that were impossible to suppress. She was grateful for the frequent interruptions of greetings from old friends. At least it helped with the flow of small-talk as she made introductions and went into explanations afterwards.

'He was head boy during my last year at school,' she chattered on after one such intro-duction.

Grant's firm fingers had somehow strayed to her wrist. 'Your pulse is going like the clappers,' he observed drily. 'Is the excitement proving too much for you?'

'For Pete's sake!' she exploded, her colour mounting, 'Can't you forget you're a doctor and just enjoy yourself?'

'Oh, but I am enjoying myself. Stop being so uptight. The last thing I want is to spoil things for you.'

'Your being here doesn't bother me one way or the other,' she retorted.

'Good!' He gave a derisory smile. 'Now I know where I stand I'll try not to bother you again.'

The dance came to an end. He escorted her back to their table, whereupon he was whisked off by her father to meet other people in the community who had known Grant's father.

Joanne seemed happy enough to have most of her time monopolised by Tony, in spite of his fall from grace over Chopin.

Bryony, on the other hand, although having plenty of invitations to dance and plenty of old acquaintances to catch up with, felt depressed and out of tune with the lively company.

It surprised her the readiness with which Grant entered into team races and square dances, even the Paul Jones. He could certainly be affable to all and sundry when he chose, she brooded resentfully. Why did he have to treat her in such a cavalier fashion?

With everyone in high spirits as they all went home together she was forced to put on a show of gaiety to match theirs. And Grant appeared genuinely to have enjoyed the evening as much as anyone.

The following morning after church Mr Clemence offered to show Grant the cemetery where his grandparents were buried and the house where his father had lived. Bryony opted to go on home to help her mother with the lunch. With the weather still beautiful, a tour of beauty spots on the moor had been planned for the afternoon.

As it turned out, on their way back for lunch Mr Clemence came across one of his ewes starting into labour with her second lambing.

'Sorry, my dears,' he told them on reaching home, 'You'll have to count me out this afternoon. My stockman's away, and I'll probably have to get the vet over.'

Bryony's mother decided to stand by, too, in case of need, and Joanne had already arranged to go riding with Tony.

'You take the shooting-brake and show Grant a few places, Bryony,' her father said. 'You know the moor as well as anyone. You could go to the Punch Bowl and Winsford Hill . . .'

It was the very thing Bryony had been hoping to avoid, but there seemed no help for it.

'Right,' she said, putting on a great show of willingness for everyone's benefit, 'I'll take you on

a magical mystery tour, Grant, and improve your
education. You don't know what a storehouse of
information I am on this part of the world. And
you'd better borrow a pair of Dad's boots. You
have to walk to see the best bits.'

'I shall look forward to having my education
improved,' he returned with mock gravity.

She actually was fairly knowledgeable about the
history of the area. She calculated that if she kept
talking, in an informative sort of way, then that
would help her to keep the heat out of the situation,
to fight this tendency of his to reduce her to a state
of nerves.

What she had not allowed for when he took his
place beside her in the brake was that he would rest
his arm along the back of her seat. Or that his eyes
would be fixed on her when they weren't on the
things she was pointing out to him.

In spite of all her chatter as they bumped over
windy moorland by ways, she grew more and more
tense. Her grip on the wheel helped to steady her to
some extent, until he remarked in mild amusement:

'Relax, girl. Anyone would think you were
wrestling with a boa constrictor!'

'You're not paying attention, are you?' she re-
proved. 'I just mentioned those old iron-mine
workings over there.'

'I heard you.'

'And up on the top of the ridge,' she pointed
away to the rounded hills, some in shadow, some in
sunlight, 'that's where the barrows are. You know,

the Bronze-age burial chambers?'

'I didn't think you meant wheelbarrows,' he returned flippantly.

She allowed herself a grin. 'Am I boring you?'

'Not at all. I'm absolutely fascinated by the sound of your voice.' He smiled the crooked smile that made her pulse-rate double and played with a tendril of hair at the back of her neck.

Bryony fidgeted. 'Please don't.' She looked at her watch, pondering, 'How much time have we got? It's too far to go to the coast or Doone country. I know, I'll take you to one of my favourite places; then we can get out and stretch our legs and you can take some more pictures for your father.'

She picked up speed and they drove for some while over the high moorland plateau with its sepia bracken, golden gorse and myriad trickling streams. Presently they dropped to a small hamlet of thatched houses. Taking a winding lane through a sheltered wooded valley brought them to a giant causeway of flat stones spanning a stretch of the full river.

'There you are, that's a bit of history. An ancient clapper bridge,' she told him. 'It's called Tarr Steps. I'm sure your father would know it. Some people say it's pre-thirteenth century.'

They left the car and wandered over to the enormous stone slabs raised on their supporting boulders across the fast-flowing water.

'Fantastic,' he murmured, 'when you think of men having to manhandle their materials all those years ago.'

The afternoon sun slanted through the trees lending a warm glow to the scene, picking out the colours of autumn. Bryony began to dawdle across the bridge, pausing to watch the shoals of tiny fish that lurked in the shallows. She was lulled to a sense of peace by the fascinating voice of the river.

Grant called her name, his camera at the ready when she turned. Then he followed her across the slabs to the other side of the water.

They strolled idly along the wild bank until they came to a spot where two streams converged. On all sides the woods rose up around them like a natural cathedral. Caught in the magic of the setting, Bryony suddenly held her breath at the sight of a massive-antlered stag. He was standing not twenty yards from them, feeding on the red berries of a rowan tree. Silently she touched Grant's arm and pointed.

'Beaut!' he murmured in admiration. He raised his camera but before he could focus, the beast glided swiftly away, disappearing into the thicket.

'Too bad!' laughed Bryony, 'but even to see one you must be especially favoured. You could look for red deer for days without any luck, although there are still lots of them about.'

'I'm especially favoured in more ways than one today.' His eyes glinted mockingly as he put an arm about her shoulders. She slipped out from under it, fearful of betraying her ever-growing attachment to him.

Turning back, she ran ahead, picking her way between tree roots and puddles, nettles and brambles, while keeping an eye open for anything else to point out. A sinuous briar across her path tripped her. She went sprawling headlong in the boggy wet grass. Angry with herself, she was scrambling to get up when an olive-green reptile reared flattened head out of the undergrowth by her hand and hissed at her.

Momentarily mesmerised, Bryony watched it slither away into the undergrowth.

Grant, at her side to help her up, saw it too. 'That was a snake!' he said sharply.

'Yes.' She gazed ruefully at the state of her muddied jacket and jeans and inspected a jagged tear on the side of her hand.

'What's this?' he rapped out, seizing the hand and examining the tear which was oozing blood.

'I-I must have caught it on a flint.'

He began to squeeze the cut to encourage the flow of blood. 'What kind of snake was it . . . did you see?'

She gave a shaky laugh. 'I don't know. A grass snake probably.'

'Could it have been an adder?'

'Could've been, I suppose. Don't Grant!' she yelled, 'You're hurting me.'

Ignoring her protest, he continued to squeeze the place before sucking hard and spitting out the blood.

'Grant, there's no need for that. Whatever it was, I wasn't bitten.'

'It spat. I saw it. You might have got some venom in there.' He eyed her anxiously before taking her arm to hurry back to the car. 'Come on, I've got my first-aid gear. Oh, blast! I haven't. Not my car, is it. We'd better get you home quickly.'

Back at the shooting-brake he thought she should let him drive.

Bryony let out a patient sigh. 'What's all the fuss? The only thing that's wrong with me is that I've ruined my clothes and you've made my hand feel ten times worse than it was. If you try to be logical, it was much more likely to have been a grass snake than an adder. It was in wet grass after all. Adders like dry places.'

He admitted she might be right. 'God! I never felt more inadequate though,' he sighed, binding the cut with the clean handkerchief she had found in her pocket. 'Here are we, miles from anywhere. I've no idea where the nearest poison bank is. And if I'd needed to cut down, the only thing I've got with me is this very unsterile object.' He produced a small pen-knife from his hip-pocket, which he said he used for any and everything.

'Thank goodness I was saved from that!' She scowled, climbing into the driving seat before he could insist on taking over.

They travelled in silence for much of the journey home, but she was ever conscious of being under observation. Grant's arm, again resting along the back of her seat, made his presence beside her far too close for comfort.

She sought to relieve the tension by saying with a light laugh: 'I'm all right, you know. There's no need for you to watch me like a hawk. I should have been feeling pretty rough by now if I *had* been bitten by a viper. But as you can see, I'm fine.'

'Your hands are trembling,' he pointed out.

'Well, I didn't know you were going to turn into a werewolf, did I?'

'Huh! And I didn't know you planned on having a mudbath. You look a sight. Your face is well-plastered. God knows what your parents will think I've been doing with you.'

'Oh, I always get to grips with nature when I come home,' she retorted airily. 'It makes a change from having to be polite to stuffy MO's at the Heathside.

He restrained a smile. 'You're a queer girl. I think you're more afraid of me than you were of that snake.'

'Don't you think it's marvellous the way stags grow those great antlers fresh every year?' she returned sweetly.

'So we change the subject when we want to evade the issue,' he murmured, half to himself.

Back at the farm they left their muddied boots in the kitchen porch before going through to where Farmer Clemence and the vet sat together, having a well-earned cup of tea.

Bryony's father roared with laughter at the sight of her. 'Good gracious, girl, did you have to scrabble on your hands and knees to find him the best bits of Exmoor?'

She laughed, easing off her muddied jacket and saying with dignity: 'A slight tumble, that was all.

*He'll* tell you all about it, I'm sure. How did the
lambing go?'

'Twins. They're both fine, and so's the old lady.'
Mr Clemence introduced Grant to the vet. 'And
here's someone else whose father might have
known your dad,' he said.

Bryony left the men to talk while she ran upstairs
to wash and change. After swapping her spoiled
clothes for a pleated skirt and a soft blue sweater,
she combed some order into her wind-whipped
curls and prepared to go down again in search of a
plaster for her hand.

On the landing she met Grant who had come up
to get his things together.

'Did you wash that well?' he asked, taking her
hand and inspecting the place.

'Of course. I'm a nurse, aren't I? I'm just going
down to get a plaster.'

He pulled her towards his room. 'I've got one
somewhere.' Finding a suitable dressing in his toilet
case, he peeled off the backing and stuck it in
position. There was a brief strange gentleness in his
eyes as he continued to hold her hand in his. 'Sorry
if I hurt you. I panicked.'

She smiled wanly. 'You can't say it wasn't an
eventful weekend.'

'On the contrary. Really action-packed from
Friday night on!'

At the reminder of Friday night she felt herself
blush. It was a welcome interruption to have Joanne come racing upstairs at that moment, to change
out of her riding gear.

When tea was over there was little time left except for a browse through some old naval photographs of the two fathers and a last riotous half-hour session on the piano between Grant and Joanne.

Then came the moment for Grant to set off back to London. He took leave of Bryony's mother with a kiss. 'Goodbye, Mrs Clemence, and thank you. It's been a grand break.'

'You must come again, dear,' she returned, 'whenever you can spare the time. How about Christmas?'

'I'll most likely be on standby then.' Grant cast a sideways glance at Bryony. 'But I doubt very much whether your daughter could be prevailed upon to bring me again.'

'I don't need to bring you now that you know the way,' said Bryony quietly.

Her father exchanged a hearty handshake with their guest. 'A pleasure to meet you, my boy. And you tell that father of yours there's always a bed for him here whenever he decides to come.' He strode towards his own car. 'Come on Bryony, we'll see him off the premises . . . put him on the right road.'

Grant was kissing Joanne goodbye and wishing her luck with her music exam. Bryony hurried after her father before she, also, could be subjected to the same treatment. She felt that if his lips touched hers once more she would no longer be able to hide her true feelings. It was an immense relief when she waved him a last farewell as they headed him in the right direction for London.

Now that he had gone, she thought, she would be able to relax and enjoy all the things she usually did on coming home. Like gathering the hens' eggs from the nest boxes, and grooming the dogs, and riding with Joanne. Like catching up on the local news, and amazing her mother with all the latest developments in the nursing world, telling her about some of the patients. But perversely all she felt for the rest of her stay was a vague discontent with life and a desire to get back to London as soon as possible. Even preparations for Christmas, when she took her turn to stir wishes into the dark pudding mixture, had less appeal than usual.

Grant's name perpetually cropped up in family conversation, until she could have screamed at the constant reminder of that maddening individual. There was no denying that in spite of his infuriating ways she was now head over heels in love with the man.

The situation was hopeless. She spent days and nights brooding about him and could think of no solution other than leaving the Royal Heathside. Perhaps if she put distance between herself and Grant she might at least have a chance of banishing him from her mind. A fresh scene, perhaps a post-grad course in something, might be the answer. And yet she was loathe to lose sight of him, although it would be nothing short of torment still to be near him when his heart was elsewhere.

'Oh, damn you, Grant Stirling,' she mourned in the small hours of a restless night, 'I was fine at the Heathside until you showed up.'

# CHAPTER SEVEN

FRIDAY morning brought Bryony's visit to an end. Normally, much as she enjoyed coming home, she had no reluctance in returning to her chosen way of life. But this time she was torn between an insane desire to be back and near to Grant, and a longing to remain within the security of home.

Today her mother and sister were driving with her to Exeter to put her on the train, after which they had planned a shopping expedition there.

'Wish I were coming shopping with you,' Bryony said with a heartfelt sigh.

'But you've got smashing shops in London,' exclaimed Joanne. 'You usually can't wait to get back to the smoke.'

Mrs Clemence cast her elder daughter a sympathetic smile. 'I know how you feel, love. I used to be exactly the same when it was time for me to go back after a holiday. You'll be all right once you get into the routine again.'

Bryony nodded. It was easier to let it be thought that she was merely suffering from an over-dose of home-sickness than that she was being a lovesick loony.

'Nearer Christmas we'll come up to London to see you,' her mother promised.

Now she had left behind the safe refuge of her

family and was journeying back to her dilemma at the Royal Heathside. The train rattled on its way, bringing her ever nearer to London but no nearer to a solution.

As she brooded over it, another complication struck her. If she did leave the Heathside, then she would have to move out of the flat. There would be no point in staying in the same neighbourhood where she might still bump into Grant. A new position would have to be in a new area, if it was going to work. And that would mean letting Judy down.

And how would she explain things to Judy? It would hardly be advisable to admit the truth. Not that Judy wouldn't understand, but she might let it slip to John. People in love often told each other things without intending to betray a confidence. Bryony couldn't bear to think of being gossiped about and pitied in the doctors' messroom.

When her train roared into Paddington station at three o'clock that afternoon she had still not been able to come to a decision about anything. She had toyed with the idea of giving in her notice at the end of the month. That way the break would come at Christmas when she could again go home for a spell. Meantime she would have to study the nursing magazines to see what other suitable posts were on offer.

Back at the flat, even the act of unpacking her case and putting away her things sent a wave of nostalgia over her at the prospect of leaving it. She couldn't help remembering all the good times that she and Judy had enjoyed and the way they had immediately warmed to each other right from their early training days.

Pulling herself together, Bryony went into the kitchen to check their duty-roster pinned on the wall. She saw that Judy would be back at five and she planned to surpise her friend with a feast.

Mrs Clemence had loaded her daughter with goodies to bring back. Unpacking the carrier Bryony found lamb chops, apple turnovers and clotted cream as well as a rich fruit gingerbread. She set about washing up the sinkful of dirty crocks before starting preparations.

She had just popped the chops into the oven when Judy drifted in at five o'clock, obviously glad to see Bryony back.

'Oh, hi!' she said, with a rather wan smile. 'I'm dying to know how you got on with His Nibs. Wait till I get out of this uniform and then you can fill me in on the nitty-gritty.' She trailed towards her bedroom, calling, 'Be a pal and make me a coffee.' When she came back in her dressing-gown she was clutching the aspirin bottle.

Making coffee for them both, Bryony registered that her friend was not her usual bright self. 'Had a bad day?'

Judy wrinkled her nose. 'Not particularly. It's the remains of this cold I've had; it's left me with a thick head.' She rubbed at her temples. 'Mind if we have the radio off?'

'Of course not.' Bryony switched off the transistor before carrying their drinks through to the living-room. 'Do you want to go and have a lie down? We can talk later.'

'Oh, no. If I do that I shan't want to get up again. I'll be all right once I've had these.' Judy tipped a couple of tablets out of the bottle and swallowed them down with sips of coffee. 'As a matter of fact, I did see Grant Stirling when he got back on Monday. He told me it had been an "interesting" weekend, whatever that meant. That was the first time he'd ever been to the west country, you know?'

Bryony nodded. 'Yes, he told me.'

'He was at Edinburgh before he came here.'

'Oh, we didn't talk about that,' said Bryony.

Judy tucked her feet up under her on the sofa. 'What did you talk about? What did you do?'

'Well, I tried to avoid heart-to-hearts with him as much as possible, seeing that we rub each other up the wrong way as easy as winking. Joanne being home made things better, they got on like a house on fire. He plays the piano pretty well which made him tops in her estimation.' Briefly she related some of the things they had done over the weekend. 'And what do you bet, when I meet him on the ward I'll just be part of the furniture!'

'Come on!' Judy exclaimed, 'Grant's not like that. I don't know what you've got against the guy.'

Bryony changed the subject. 'I hope you're hungry, because it's big eats tonight.'

When the meal was put in front of her Judy was duly appreciative, although she had difficulty in doing justice to it. 'Do you mind if I save my dessert for tomorrow, Bry? Think I will turn in now, if you don't mind. I'm on an early again tomorrow. And so are you, aren't you?' She yawned and shuffled off towards the bathroom. 'Don't let me oversleep, will you?'

It suited Bryony to be left to her own devices for the time being, since it saved her from having to talk about Grant Stirling. After clearing away the remains of their meal, she settled down for a leisurely evening. She washed her hair, filed her nails and was about to look out a clean uniform for the morning when, at nine o'clock, the doorbell shrilled.

Promptly she went to answer it, to avoid a second blast disturbing Judy. On the doorstep she found John Dawson and Mike Tavistock.

'Missed you, Light of my Life!' declared Mike, going down on one knee and throwing his arms wide. 'I've come to carry you away on my milk-white Spitfire.'

She giggled. 'Come in, both of you.'

John grinned, digging his hands into his pockets. 'Actually we thought you two might like to come out for a drink. Where is Judy?'

'Gone to bed, I'm afraid, John. She was feeling whacked.' Bryony led the way into the living-room.

'Oh!' John sounded disappointed. 'It would probably have bucked her up to come out. Mike's found this great new wine bar near St Benedict's. See if she's asleep, will you?'

Bryony went to look, cautiously opening her friend's door and as cautiously closing it again.

'She's well away. It wouldn't be fair to wake her. You'll have to share me between you.'

Sitting in the front of the car with Mike and with John leaning over her shoulder, Bryony asked how they came to be frequenting bars in the neighbourhood of the other hospital.

Mike laid a finger against one side of his nose. 'The heart hath its reasons, my darling.'

'Mike!' she exclaimed. 'You wouldn't be thinking of poaching on Grant Stirling's preserves?'

'If by that you mean am I dogging the footsteps of the adorable Vivien, you may be right. As a matter of fact,' he confided, 'they had this bazaar at St Benny's last Saturday and I actually got talking to her.' He sighed ecstatically. 'Sadly, she had plans for that evening and me being knocked for six, like a dope, I didn't think to get her phone number.'

Bryony groaned and exchanged a despairing glance with John. 'Aren't there enough strings to your bow without you queering someone else's pitch? Besides, I wouldn't care to step on Grant Stirling's toes.'

'He doesn't own the girl,' said Mike obstinately. 'Besides, all's fair in love and war.'

They were approaching St Benedict's when they saw her coming off-duty, a neat figure with her auburn hair framing her navy blue outdoors uniform cap.

'There she is!' cried Mike. 'Oh, blast!' he fumed as the traffic lights forced him to pull up.

Although he hooted, she didn't glance in their direction. They watched her stepping purposefully across the road to where another car waited to pick her up.

Bryony was beginning to know the sleek, silver lines of that car. John also recognised it as it passed them on the other side of the road. 'And that, my dear Mike, was Grant,' he observed, 'whether he owns her or not.'

Mike scowled. 'Shall we follow them?'

'Don't be silly.' Bryony gave a nervous laugh. 'What about this fabulous wine-bar you're supposed to be taking me to? I don't want to spend the evening chasing after your next *affaire d'amour*.'

'You're right,' he grinned, 'Keep 'em waiting, that's the best way,' and he carried on towards their original destination.

Presently they were all three seated around a huge wine barrel, sampling a brew from the cask in a pseudo-Elizabethan setting, complete with sawdust on the floor and torch-like lanterns on the wall. But despite the convivial atmosphere, after an initial spurt of conversation they lapsed into mournful monosyllables.

'If I'd known I was in for such a stimulating time I mightn't have come,' declared Bryony.

'Things on our minds, love,' Mike said. 'There's John missing his Judy, and me broody over a redhead. But what's your excuse for the vapours?'

'Just the thought of work after a week's holiday,' she returned with a grimace, 'and since I'm on at seven-thirty in the morning, would you mind if we called it a day?'

Even after her early night Judy was still feeling far from well the following morning. 'I've still got this headache,' she complained, 'and my throat's a bit sore.'

'Take the day off,' said Bryony. 'They can get an agency nurse if they're short.'

'Oh, I'll probably forget it when I'm working,' Judy decided, and they went in to work together.

Up on Addison Ward Bryony received the report from the night staff while breakfasts were being served. Later, having caught up on all the happenings in her absence, she went round to see all her patients, old and new.

In the male High Dependency area she now found Mr Gladwin, back from Intensive Care and making good progress towards recovery from his collapse. Heartened at the satisfactory outcome of their efforts on that frenzied evening, she lingered by his bedside to exchange a few cheerful words.

She was about to move on when he said, with a little hesitation, 'Er, Sister, can I tell you something?'

'Yes, Mr Gladwin?' she smiled, 'What is it?'

He rubbed his nose, looking embarrassed. 'You'll probably think me a queer cove, but remember when I was brought in here after that accident, and I had this turn? Well, I passed right out, didn't I?'

'You did.'

He gazed at her, bright-eyed. 'You might've thought I didn't know what was going on. But I could see meself lying flat on that bed, and I could hear voices, and I knew yours, Sister.'

'Did you?' She expressed surprise, although well aware that she should not be. It was a fact that even if people appeared to be unconscious, they could quite often hear what was going on around them.

'Yes. You squeezed my hand, didn't you, and your voice was like a candle in the dark to me. I knew you wouldn't let me go, not if you could help it. I just latched onto that. Next thing I knew I was in the other ward. Just thought I'd like you to know, and to say thank you, Sister.'

The warmth in his eyes made her swallow against the lump in her throat.

'That's why we're here, Mr Gladwin, but it was nice of you to tell me. I'm glad you're so much better. Not long now and you'll be going home.'

She went on to see Colin Goddard, their young epileptic, whose outlook by contrast was sad. During her absence he had deteriorated rapidly. The previous night had seen him lapse into a coma.

Patty Newman was there with another nurse, attending to the boy's pressure areas. She was looking very depressed and she had obviously been weeping.

Over the time since Colin's condition had been diagnosed Patty had built up quite a rapport with him. She had taken and collected him from radiotherapy and been a good friend in many ways, always keeping a cheerful face although she knew the prognosis was grave.

Now Bryony drew her to one side and attempted

to encourage her. 'It had to come, Patty,' she murmured. 'Be glad for him that this happened so quickly. He'll be out of pain now. He could've lingered for months. You did your best for him, didn't you?'

'Yes, Sister. Thank you, Sister.' Patty gulped and ran for the sluice room.

Bryony stayed to help the other nurse finish the treatment and put up the cot sides. Then she blew her own nose and drew a deep breath before crossing over to the women's side.

In the female High Dependency unit Tina Vincent, still on bed rest, was making a great fuss over being required to drink a glass of Complan.

'Oh, Sister, must I drink this horrible stuff? I'm full up. I had a huge breakfast. I'm positively bloated.'

Bryony laughed. 'Oh no, you're not. It only feels like that. Toss it down, there's a good girl. You've been doing very well, I hear.'

Tina frowned and put on a pained face as she sipped. 'I'll never get into any of my clothes again.'

'So look on the bright side. When you go home you can go on a shopping spree and buy a whole new wardrobe.'

'And have my mother creating like mad,' moaned the girl.

'She'll be so glad to have you well again, I'm sure she won't.' Bryony fervently hoped she was right. 'Anyway, once you're fit you can get around to earning your own living, can't you? Any ideas what you'd like to do?'

Tina shrugged and looked a little shy. 'We-ell, since I've been in here I was wondering if I might be a nurse?'

'Oh, really?' Bryony was pleasantly surprised although not totally convinced. 'Well, I don't see why you shouldn't be, once you've built up some muscles. I should send away for some literature. It'll give you something to aim for.'

The woman in the bed opposite chimed in: 'I forgive 'er for borrowing my coat that time. She's a case, isn't she? Still, it was nice of her mum to send me those chocolates, even though I can't eat 'em with my complaint. I gave 'em to the nurses.'

Bryony smiled. 'And who sent you these?' she asked, putting her nose to the lovely red roses on Tina's locker.

'It was my brother's friend, Dave. *You* know.'

'Oh yes, the guy who was with you in Carlo's. I hear he's been phoning regularly. He's asking if he can come in and see you. Would you like to see him?'

Tina fingered a strand of her wispy dark hair. 'I might.'

'Speak to Dr Stirling. If you continue to be good and eat your quota, he may let him come.'

She went on to the next patient, glad to be back and busy with other people's problems. That was the best antidote she knew for forgetting her own troubles.

So far since her return Bryony had not set eyes on Grant. With Sister McCullagh coming on duty at one o'clock it was she who accompanied the registrar on his afternoon round, while Bryony stayed in the treatment room helping a junior nurse to dress a varicose ulcer. When that was finished it seemed an opportune moment to check their stocks of sterile packs which seemed to be getting low. It also kept Bryony conveniently out of Grant's way.

Afternoon tea was being brought to the patients when Bryony saw the senior sister return to her office alone. She presumed the round must be finished and the registrar gone, and she prepared to join Sister McCullagh in the office to catch up on any new developments.

On the way she was suddenly confronted by Grant Stirling who emerged from Tina Vincent's room.

Her pulse began its usual clamouring as he barred her passage, saying: 'Good afternoon, Bryony. Would I be right in thinking you were making yourself scarce today?'

She made herself meet his unwavering gaze. 'No! Why should I do that? I happened to be busy.'

Raised eyebrows plainly said he did not believe her. 'How's this?' He reached for her hand to examine the remains of her cut.

'Fine, as you can see. It didn't prove fatal!'

The ghost of a smile curved his lips. 'That was a good weekend I had.'

'I'm glad you enjoyed it.'

'You have a delightful family. It almost makes one change one's mind.'

'About what?' she asked.

'The slippery straits of matrimony.' There was a glint of mockery in his eyes as he studied her.

Bryony's returning smile was wintry. 'Are you a misogynist? Dear me, poor Vivien. Someone should warn her.'

'Oh, Vivien knows where she's going. She doesn't need your pity.'

'I pity her sincerely if she's to be tied to a—a—cynic like you,' flashed Bryony, and as instantly wished she had held her tongue.

The teasing in his eyes faded. 'Do you indeed?'

She looked at her shoes to avoid his stern gaze. 'I-I'm sorry. I shouldn't have said that. It's none of my business.'

'You're too right, it isn't!' He stalked away, his lips tight with anger.

The interlude left her heavy-hearted and wretched. Why must she always fight with him when her inclinations were the exact opposite? The friction between them was making her life at the Heathside unendurable. Continuing on her way to the office, she finally made up her mind to leave. It was the only way to rescue herself from this running battle between them.

In spite of his cutting attitude, there was no denying to herself that this mortifying man had her completely enthralled; which was a bittersweet hell when his own affections were elsewhere. And by their many clashes he had demonstrated only too convincingly that he utterly despised her by this time.

Bryony felt abject with misery. If only they could

have been friends it might have been bearable; she could at least have continued to adore him in secret. Her life at the Heathside had once been absorbing and fulfilling, with its fair share of fun, but since the day that Grant Stirling had crossed the threshold it had become one great whirlpool of difficulties. She would give in her notice at the end of the month, there was nothing else for it.

Back in the office, having pulled herself together, she discussed with Sister McCullagh the new treatments ordered and the patients for discharge. Then the senior sister went off to tea leaving Bryony to carry on supervising the work of the ward.

Colin Goddard's mother sought her out for a talk on her son's condition. In the circumstances Mrs Goddard was bearing up nobly. Afterwards Bryony reflected how brave some people were in the face of misfortune, the unsung heroes and heroines of everyday life. And yet here was she, preparing to run away in order to save her sanity.

There remained the problem of what to tell Judy. During the day she had seen nothing of her friend since they'd parted company in the morning, but they would be meeting up again when they both went off duty at four-thirty.

Sister McCullagh was taking a phone call as Bryony was about to leave. 'Just a moment, dear,' she called, her round face creased with concern. 'We're having an admission . . . a member of staff. You share a flat with Judy Perrin, don't you?'

'Yes. You don't mean . . . it's Judy who's coming

in?' A shaft of fear went through Bryony. 'She did have a bad head last night and this morning. Why . . . what's happened?'

'Pyrexia, rigors, vomiting,' Sister McCullagh spread her hands and shrugged. 'Could be a number of things. Stirling spoke about a lumbar puncture. She's coming up now; I thought you might like to be around.'

'Oh yes, thank you.' Bryony's voice was choked, her throat suddenly dry as possible causes occurred to her.

'Come on, we'd better make sure that sideroom's ready.' The older woman bustled along the corridor leaving Bryony to follow. Her hands were damp with apprehension. She sent up a silent prayer that it wouldn't be anything as dire as polio. Could it be something she'd eaten?

All was in readiness to receive Judy when they brought her up on a stretcher. Bryony was shocked to find her friend confused and delirious, her mutterings unintelligible. She hunched herself into a ball on the bed, protesting feebly as they undressed her, screwing her eyes against the light.

Sister McCullagh, talking pulse and temperature, drew in her breath sharply. Bryony shaded the bed-light so that it did not shine into Judy's eyes, then she sponged the burning face with a cool cloth.

'Judy? It's me, Bryony,' she murmured comfortingly, but there was no recognition from her friend.

As soon as they had got her settled Grant Stirling

arrived, bringing with him Sir Phineas Forbes who had happened to be in the building. Urbane and professional in immaculate black jacket and striped trousers, he was a very different Sir Phineas from the night of the party. .

With a brief word of greeting to the sisters, he stepped to the bedside with Grant. Together they made their careful observations, testing various reflexes, putting occasional questions to Bryony, which she did her best to answer.

Finally Sir Phineas straightened his tall frame and stroked his chin thoughtfully. 'I think you may be right, Grant,' he pronounced, 'it appears to be a meningeal virus we have here, but we can't be sure until we get it confirmed by lumbar puncture. We'll do that now, shall we?'

Slipping off his jacket, he handed it to Bryony with a brief smile. 'Will you look after that for me, my dear?' Then he rolled up the sleeves of his pristine white shirt and went to the sink to scrub up.

Sister McCullagh had ready the trolley with sterile equipment. Bryony stayed by her friend, holding her hand.

She would have moved as sterile towels were laid on the bottom sheet, preparing the bed for the vital procedure, but Grant detained her. 'No, you stay there with her, although I don't think she knows too much about anything at the moment.'

So Bryony cradled the sick girl's head in her arms while the doctors pinpointed the site for the extraction of spinal fluid. Grant gave the local anaesthetic and Sir Phineas duly performed the lumbar puncture.

'There you are, that's all over,' he said in a brisk manner. 'Rush this through Path Lab, and then we can decide on treatment.' He passed the syringe to Grant to take the appropriate specimens for analysis.

After he had washed his hands once more, Bryony helped the great man into his jacket again. 'Thank you, my dear.' He gave her a fatherly pat on the shoulder. 'It shouldn't take too long to get the results.'

Both doctors departed, discussing their patient in earnest tones. Exchanging anxious glances, Bryony and Sister McCullagh straightened the bedclothes of the sick Judy and put up the cot sides. Grant Stirling had himself taken the specimens for the Path Lab, so there was little they could do but wait.

'Does her mother know yet?' Bryony asked.

Sister McCullagh wrinkled her forehead. 'I don't think so. Her collapse was so sudden, and there was no reply when they rang her home. Do you know Mrs Perrin?' When Bryony nodded, she went on, 'You have another try, then. It'll be less alarming coming from you. And better tell her to come prepared to spend the night if possible.' Heaving a deep sigh Sister McCullagh prepared to clear up the used equipment. 'Oh dear, I hope they get a move on with those tests.'

'With Dr Stirling on the job you can be sure of that,' returned Bryony with confidence. She recal-

led Judy's earlier remark about wishing for someone like Grant to be around if ever she needed
emergency treatment. Well, she had got her wish,
and Bryony felt profoundly grateful for his presence in the hospital. If there was anything to be
done for Judy, then Grant could be relied upon to
see to it.

Going to the telephone she was lucky enough to
contact Mrs Perrin who had just come in from
work. Finding the right words to break the news
wasn't easy, but she managed to convey the
seriousness of the matter without sounding too
alarmist.

'If you can manage to stay the night, Mrs Perrin,
we do have a visitors' room on the ward. Better to
be here on the spot than worrying at home on your
own, isn't it? Yes, I'll still be here when you come.'

Bryony went back to keep vigil with her friend in
the darkened sideward. Lively, high-spirited Judy,
now lying almost comatose between her vague
meanderings, stricken down by some mysterious
bug.

Dear God, please, oh please let those tests be
benign, she prayed.

It was seven-thirty before Judy's widowed
mother arrived, scared but making an effort to be
brave. They stayed for a while talking quietly by
Judy's bed, until Sister McCullagh suggested that
Bryony should take Mrs Perrin down to the canteen
for a meal.

'Judy's had a sedative,' she said, 'and there's
nothing more we can do until we get those results.'

Down in the canteen they were shortly joined by Mike Tavistock, for once in his life not being flippant as he enquired how Judy was faring. Bryony made the introductions.

'Your daughter's in the right place, Mrs Perrin,' Mike said, trying to be reassuring. 'Addison's a great ward. She'll get five-star treatment up there, don't you worry. Old John's going to kick himself he wasn't around. Had the day off to go to Oxford for an interview,' he went on to explain. 'Maybe he's better off than the rest of us; at least we should know what's cooking by the time he gets back. Be seeing you, Bry,' and he left them to their meal.

Mrs Perrin endeavoured to push down the egg and chips which Bryony had persuaded her to try. 'Will you be going back to the flat after this?' she asked, leaving what she could not eat.

'Oh, Lord, no. I couldn't go home before we have some news. I'll stay on with you for a bit.' She gathered up their plates. 'I'll get us some coffee.'

Afterwards, with her arm linked through Mrs Perrin's as they made their way back to the ward, Bryony endeavoured to strike a cheerful note. But she knew that even with the most favourable diagnosis there was a tough battle ahead for Judy.

The night staff had taken over by the time Grant returned to the ward with the vital information. In the company of the night sister he came to the sideward and motioned Bryony outside.

'The spinal fluid confirms viral meningitis,' he said in a low voice. 'Bad enough, but not as bad as it might have been. With any luck and no complications, she'll be okay.'

Bryony swallowed hard. It was true, things might have been much worse. Now they knew what they were dealing with, aided by modern drugs, there was every hope that her friend would make a complete recovery. 'Thank you.' She drew a tremulous breath. 'Yes, it could have been worse.' She nodded to Mrs Perrin, sitting by the bedside. 'That's her mother . . . will you tell her?'

'Of course.' Accompanied by the duty sister he went towards the anxious mother with a kindly smile and a handclasp.

As Byrony heard his deep, gentle voice offering comfort and reassurance where needed, her carefully preserved self-control threatened to break. She hurried for privacy, seeking refuge in the linen room, and laying her head against a stack of clean sheets, she cried her heart out.

It was a few minutes later when she felt a firm hand on her shoulder and heard the deep voice, still gentle, saying: 'I guess this has been tough on you.'

'Oh!' she exclaimed in confusion as she turned to see Grant and strove to halt her tears. But they would not stop and she turned away again, feeling in her pocket for a dry tissue.

'Here you are.' He put a folded handkerchief into her hand.

She shook it out, mopped her eyes and blew her nose. 'Th-thank you. St-stupid of me . . . but I'm very close to Judy.'

He turned her round to face him, lifting her

tragic face with one finger and subjecting her to a searching gaze. But his eyes were not steely now, they were kind. 'You must look after yourself, young lady. I should push off now and leave it to the night staff.'

She bit her quivering lips. 'B-but I . . .' she began.

'You can't spend all day and night at the bedside. You're on duty tomorrow?'

She nodded.

'We shall have you cracking up too, if you can't be sensible. There are other nurses quite capable of looking after Judy. We're starting her on strep-tomycin. I understand her mother is staying, so she's not being neglected. Off home with you now. And take a couple of something to help you sleep.'

He left her to regain her self-control.

# CHAPTER EIGHT

THE telephone was ringing as Bryony arrived back at the flat that night. Answering it, she heard John's voice at the other end of the line.

'Hi, Bryony!' He sounded bright. 'Judy there?'

'Oh, John,' she returned with a deep sigh, 'where are you?'

'At my place . . . I've just got back.'

'So you haven't heard yet?'

There was a pause before he said: 'I haven't seen anyone. Heard what?'

Bryony hesitated. 'Well, perhaps you'd better ring Grant, or Mike. Judy's on Addison . . . she's been warded.'

'Why? Oh, come on, Bryony, spit it out. What's going on?'

'Well, I'm sorry to have to tell you this, but Grant and Sir Phineas saw her this afternoon, and it's been confirmed as viral meningitis.'

'Oh God!' he breathed. 'I'll get straight over there.'

Poor John, she thought, as she put the phone down. And he had seemed so happy when he first came on.

Having promised to take in Judy's toilet things and night-clothes the next day, Bryony went to her friend's bedroom and promptly tripped over her outsized doggy pyjama case on the floor. She picked it up. The room was a total mess, but that was not unusual when they had an early start. Before going to bed she set about to tidy it up, which at least made her feel a little more useful.

Surprisingly, Bryony slept fairly well and awoke the following morning more able to face the day. She was not on early shift, but she went in early all the same to be with Mrs Perrin.

In the quiet sideward with Judy's mother she found Grant, who was answering her questions with sympathetic patience. So far there had been no response to treatment. Judy had spent a poor night, her temperature remaining ominously high in spite of antibiotics.

'It takes time,' Grant explained. 'There's really not a lot of point in your staying around at this stage, Mrs Perrin. You'd be better off keeping yourself busy. We should call you at once if it were necessary.'

Judy's mother hesitated. 'Well, I do have some things to see to at home. I came out in such a rush. I left my dog with a neighbour . . . and I'll have to let them know at work.'

Bryony had an inspiration. 'Why not come and stay in our flat for a few days? It would be more convenient for popping in and out of here. You could bring the dog as well . . . Sparky's no bother, is he?'

'That sounds like a sensible idea to me,' remarked Grant. 'Good for both of you.'

He went on his way as Sister McCullagh and another nurse arrived to give Judy a tepid sponging.

'Thank you, Bryony,' Mrs Perrin said, 'I think that would be a great help.'

'Okay, then. Judy's key is in her shoulder-bag, you'll find. Just come and go as you like.'

Leaving Mrs Perrin to have a word with Sister McCullagh, Bryony made for the canteen and an early lunch before starting duty.

The next seven days were anxious ones for them all while Judy hovered in a twilight world of her own, seeming to make little headway. Bryony tried not to think about the complications which might arise.

On duty she had other patients who needed their proper share of her attention, but off duty she spent as much time as possible watching over her friend. With Mr Gladwin's remarks fresh in mind, she always greeted Judy gently by name whether there was any awareness or not.

Mrs Perrin had moved in with Bryony for the time being and, as Grant had said, the arrangement worked with advantage to them both, giving each less time to brood. The little Yorkshire terrier, Sparky, was an added diversion, always providing a welcome for whoever reached home first.

With news about Judy gradually filtering through the hospital, Bryony was touched by the concern shown by everyone, for herself as well as for her friend. Mike was particularly good to her, popping round to the flat whenever he happened to be free.

'He's nice, Bryony,' Judy's mother remarked after meeting him one evening. 'Is that where your future lies?'

'Heavens, no.' Bryony shook her head with a fond smile. 'Mike's too much of a rolling stone for me. We're just mates.'

Judy's illness had pushed all thoughts of her own future out of her head. Now it struck her forcibly that if she left the Royal Heathside she would also be cutting herself off from other people, as well as Grant Stirling.

The atmosphere between Grant and herself on the ward was now co-operative and cordial. They were both far too concerned to bicker. Bryony couldn't help reflecting how ironic it was that it should take Judy's misfortune to bring about this state of affairs.

Judy was being visited daily by Grant and John. Sir Phineas also looked in twice while Bryony was on duty. She found him less intimidating since the party and he was extremely courteous to her.

On the eighth day Judy's condition began to respond to treatment. Her eyes were able to tolerate the light and her temperature began to steady. All the staff breathed a sigh of relief. Even Tina Vincent, usually engrossed with her own problems, seemed uplifted by the news.

That Sunday afternoon Bryony strolled with Mike and Mrs Perrin's little Yorkie on the heath, enjoying the wintry sunshine. 'I've never had anyone so close to me quite so sick before,' she confided, feeling as though a great weight had been lifted from her.

Mike's arm was around her shoulders and he gave her a squeeze. 'Makes you feel pretty small fry, doesn't it? Here today and gone tomorrow, and sometimes not a thing you can do about it. Grab happiness where you can, old thing, that's what I say.'

Turning her head, she gave him a swift, laughing peck on the cheek. 'And you certainly believe in practising what you preach.'

It was at that precise moment that a loud toot from a silver car on the road crossing the heath made them both glance towards it. Grant Stirling gave them a careless wave in passing.

'There goes your secret passion,' said Mike.

Bryony frowned at him and snapped: 'What a stupid thing to say.'

'Hey! No need to bite my head off,' he returned, 'I'm your mate.' His eyebrows narrowed as he gave her a curious glance. 'Don't tell me I touched a live wire? It's not the pair of us suffering from unrequited love?'

'No. Only you,' said Bryony with a short laugh. God! Was she that transparent? She would have to put on a better show.

'That's good,' Mike went on, 'and I'm working at it.'

Bryony looked at him, but left it at that.

By the end of the second week Grant pronounced himself well pleased with Judy's progress. Her temperature was stable, her headache quite gone. It became a pleasure to visit her when she was able to sit up and take a new interest in life.

There was no need now for Mrs Perrin to continue staying at the flat. She moved back to her own house again with Sparky, to pick up the threads of her own life.

To Bryony, who had sometimes wondered if she would ever see the old Judy back on form, hearing her old sense of humour and laughter returning was like a miracle. She felt thankful beyond words. Her joy embraced everyone, even Grant, despite the fact that he did seem to have become rather more distant again since that day he had seen her with Mike on the heath.

On Addison Ward, while Judy grew stronger, Colin Goddard grew steadily weaker. It was the Friday before Judy was due to leave for convalescence in the country that the boy finally slipped away, peacefully, in his sleep.

Talking with a resigned Sister McCullagh after they had both done their best to console his parents, Bryony said: 'I'm glad that Patty Newman is on days off. She'll be sorry, but an empty bed might be easier to face than the reality. She'd got quite fond of Colin.'

Sister McCullagh's forehead wrinkled reflectively. 'That's one of the hazards of this game. She'll have to come to terms with it sooner or later.'

On Saturday morning Bryony waited with Judy for the ambulance to collect her. There had been a flow of people in and out to wish her goodbye. One of the visitors had been Tina, who was herself waiting to be collected for her first day out.

'Looks a bit different from that day she collapsed in Carlo's, doesn't she?' said Judy, her eyes on the anorexic girl's slight figure. She was looking quite attractive in a warm red sweater dress which concealed her still thin frame.

'Yes,' agreed Bryony, 'but she's got a long way to go yet. She is co-operating though, which is why Grant is letting her out.' She smiled dryly. 'I think she'd do anything for him; he's become a kind of father figure.'

'And this guy Dave taking an interest in her,' put in Judy, 'that must help. Expect she feels she matters now. Great, isn't it, when things go right.'

Bryony nodded but looked regretful. 'A pity we couldn't do anything for poor young Colin.'

'You can't win 'em all, Bry. Funny how you get a new angle on things, being on the receiving end for a change,' Judy went on more cheerfully. 'I've done a lot of thinking since I nearly lost one of my nine lives.'

'What do you remember about those early days of your illness?' Bryony asked curiously.

'Not a lot, except that people and voices seemed ever so tiny and far away, like a lot of little pin-men. Anyway, as I was about to say, I've decided I've had my fill of emergencies. Think I'd like to get back to "proper" nursing, as you call it. Better to see patients recover and go home than to send battered bodies to Rose Cottage, or pass the survivors on for someone else to care for.'

Bryony chuckled. 'So glad our ministrations didn't put you off hospitals altogether.'

Her friend looked demure. 'And me going to be a doctor's wife?'

Bryony's eyebrows shot up. 'A what?'

'We-ell, John sort of proposed last night. Or as much of a proposal as I'll ever get out of him. He's short-listed for a registrar's job at Oxford, and he's asked me if I'll get a job down that way, if it comes off. He's not wildly romantic,' Judy grinned, 'but I gathered he can't bear the thought of life without me.'

'So you're going to, of course?' Bryony was delighted. 'Was it you being ill brought him to the point?'

'Maybe. My one regret is that it'll mean you and me splitting up. I hated having to tell you, really. Sorry, Bry. Who else will you ask to share?'

Wasn't this just the opportunity she'd been waiting for? Bryony mused. It was almost like fate giving her the way out. 'Well, actually, I have been thinking of moving on myself. We've been at the Heathside long enough. You can get stuck in a place . . . but I didn't want to let you down.' She gave a short laugh. 'My mother always says things work themselves out in time.'

Judy expressed surprise. 'You're a dark horse. I thought you loved it on Addison?'

'I did. Until Grant Stirling arrived.' Bryony spoke without thinking.

Frowning, Judy shook her head at a loss. 'You two need your heads banging together,' she said.

Confidences came to an end with Nurse Smith appearing on the scene to say that the ambulance had come for Judy. Others of the staff gathered to bid her goodbye and she was soon on her way amid a wealth of good wishes.

Back at the flat that evening Bryony felt forlorn, in spite of receiving a letter from home. She missed Judy's mother and the dog. She seemed to have lost touch with other friends during her preoccupation with Judy's illness. Even Mike had been less in evidence over the past week.

Bryony decided to ring him to ask him round for a meal. After all, she did owe him a few favours.

His phone was answered by a female voice with a slight brogue. 'Oh, Mike's not here at the moment, but he'll be back soon. Will I get him to call you?'

'Oh, no. It's nothing special. Just say it was Bryony called. I'll see him around.'

She put the telephone down with a thoughtful air, quite certain she knew that voice. It was Vivien's. So what was Mike up to? Well, it was nothing to do with her. And if Grant was so sure of himself, maybe he deserved to lose her.

Not wanting to bother cooking for herself, Bryony decided on something from the Chinese take-away. She pulled a heavy sweater over her jeans and set out for the lighted High Street. Rounding a corner into the main road, she suddenly caught sight of the husky figure of the registrar.

Hands in pockets, he was studying the menu framed outside the dimly-lit Chinese café.

*Oh no!* she thought in dismay, pulling up sharply. She made to cross the road to avoid him, but he looked up and saw her.

'Hi, there!' he called. 'Where are you off to?'

'Oh, er . . . I've just been to the post,' she fibbed.

'Have you eaten yet?'

Caught off-guard, she wavered, her mind filling with images of Mike and Vivien probably eating together. She wondered if Grant had any idea.

'I take it that hesitation means you haven't,' he went on briskly. 'Will you keep me company?'

'We-ell, all right. Provided we go Dutch.'

'After your parents' hospitality to me? Rubbish. Let's find somewhere decent. We'll give the chopsticks a miss tonight.' He took possession of her hand, striding along so that she had to hurry to keep up.

'But I'm not dressed for anywhere decent,' she panted.

Making for the very up-market King's Hotel, he glanced down briefly at her jeans and jersey. 'You'd pass muster in sackcloth.'

It was the closest he had ever come to paying her a compliment. She smoothed a hand over her wind-blown curls as the head waiter showed them to a discreet alcove table set with snowy linen and lighted with a small orange-shaded lamp.

'There,' said Grant, seated opposite her and smiling, 'no-one to see you except me, and I'm finding the view quite agreeable.'

'Well, I'm going to be too warm in this.' Confident in the knowledge of having a tidy blue-checked shirt underneath, she started to peel off the Arran sweater. There was no trouble in getting out of the sleeves, but as she made to take the rest of it over her head a strand of wool caught itself around the winder of her wristwatch, and there she was with her head enveloped.

'Oh, damn,' she exclaimed in a muffled voice, 'I'm stuck. Could you help me, please?'

Grant came round the table to oblige. 'Hold still a minute.' His cool hands were on her wrist, sorting out the problem and presently she was freed. 'Better take it right off before it happens again.' He unfastened the bracelet and slipped it over her hand. 'Right.'

'Thank you.' Emerging to see Grant's amused expression opposite her, she had never felt such an idiot as she bundled the jersey on the seat beside her and smoothed her ruffled hair again.

'You do get yourself into some odd situations, don't you?' he remarked, laughter in his voice.

Only when *you're* around, she thought. But aloud she said primly, 'I usually get longer notice for a dinner date.'

She was glad of the taped music softly playing; her heart was beating such a tattoo that she wondered if he might hear it.

Hovering discreetly, a waiter presented them each with a large menu and collected the woolly to hang it up.

In her confusion she could hardly see what she

was reading, so she settled for the least complicated meal she could think of; asparagus soup, followed by a cut off the roast beef joint, with mushrooms and Yorkshire pudding.

'The same for me,' Grant told the waiter, 'and we'll have a bottle of your best sparkling Burgundy.' He motioned her to hold out her hand so that he could re-fasten the wristwatch. 'This is something of a celebration, isn't it . . . your best friend back from the jaws of death?'

She smiled at him. 'That's true, and thanks for your part in it.'

He shook his head, leaning back against the red leather upholstery, taking his ease. 'Team effort. By the way, John Dawson tells me he's landed a registrar's post, starting in the new year.'

'Oh, he got it, did he?' Bryony enthused.

'He says it may mean that Judy won't be returning to the Heathside. You're going to miss her.'

'Mmm,' returned Bryony, non-committally.

'It was your friend Mike, you know, who discovered Judy that day, on the point of collapse. I must confess my opinion of him has improved with acquaintance.'

Bryony wondered if his opinion would change again if he knew who Mike was with that evening. In a contrary way she felt sorry that Grant might be in for a rude awakening.

'So where is the great lover tonight?' Grant asked, regarding her with a wry smile.

'Meaning who?' demanded Bryony.

'Mike, of course. Now that you are free again, so

to speak, I should have thought he would have seized his chance to catch up on lost time?'

She frowned, returning sharply, 'I've told you before, *I'm* not his keeper.'

Grant held up a conciliatory hand. 'All right, all right! No need to blow up.'

'I was not blowing up.'

He put on a penitent expression. 'Pax?'

She had to laugh. 'Don't start all that again! I should have built up some immunity to you by this time. I'm really a peaceful person, you know. I don't fight with anyone else.'

'Strange,' he murmured, seasoning the soup that had arrived. 'A psychologist could doubtless give us a good reason for that. I'll have to consult a buddy of mine.'

'It's hardly that important. Probably our genes just aren't sympathetic.'

He seemed about to add something more, and then apparently changed his mind and got on with his soup, afterwards turning the conversation to talk of the Devon weekend. 'My pictures came out rather well.'

'I had a letter from home, and my mother was pleased with those you sent them. I should like to have seen them.'

'You'll see them when you go home, unless . . .' he paused and went on with some diffidence, 'unless you'd care to come back to my flat. I haven't posted the copies off to my father yet.'

Bryony remembered that Mike and Grant now lived in the same block of flats. And Vivien was with Mike. She had no wish to risk bumping into them. 'Oh no,' she said quickly, 'I ought to get back. I have things to do. Some other time perhaps.'

He gave her a straight look. 'As you wish.'

She could tell that he was put out, but there was little she could do about it, except to ask him in for a quick coffee after the meal, just to show no ill-feeling.

When he had walked her the short distance to her flat, he saved her the problem by wishing her an almost curt goodnight on the pavement, so that she was relieved not to have mentioned anything about coming in.

Mulling over the strange evening, Bryony spent a restless night. It was no mystery to *her* why she always reacted so violently towards Grant. It was her self-defence mechanism taking over, saving her making a fool of herself. Because although Grant awakened all kinds of primitive desires in her, it was quite clear that he had not the slightest interest in her as a woman. And so the sooner she removed herself from contact with him, the better.

On Monday morning Bryony handed in her written resignation to Miss Davison, the Chief Nursing Officer.

'Oh dear,' Miss Davison sighed, 'we'll be sorry to lose you, Sister Clemence. I suppose you've got something else in mind?'

Bryony had to admit that she had not so far made other arrangements. 'I'm feeling the need for a break,' she explained. 'I'm going to spend some time at home before starting something else.'

Accepting this decision with some reluctance, Miss Davison said: 'Well, if your mind's made up it's no use trying to dissuade you. But remember, we should always be pleased to see you back.'

'Thank you,' said Bryony. 'I'm sorry to be going, but . . . I think it's the right course for me at present.'

The tall, spare figure of Sir Phineas Forbes was about to enter the office as she left it. Giving her a courtly bow when she held the door for him, he thanked her. And although Sir Phineas, the consultant, still inspired a certain reverence in her, she wondered why she had ever thought of him as formidable.

Later that day she saw him again when he visited Addison ward in the company of John Dawson. The new patient in Judy's place had a respiratory problem and Sir Phineas's opinion had been sought. Bryony attended the doctors, producing sphygmomanometer, spatulas and other items which were called for.

There followed a brief discussion of the case in the doctor's office. Finally the consultant said:

'A bronchogram first, I think, John. Get the lady down to X-ray. And now, if you'll excuse me a moment, I'd like a private word with Sister Clemence.'

John left the office, and as Sir Phineas motioned her to a chair Bryony had no idea what he could want with her.

Leaning on the desk with his finger-tips touching, the consultant eyed her quizzically. 'I hear from Miss Davison that you are leaving the hospital?'

Bryony was surprised that he should be interested. 'That's right, sir. I shall be going at the end of the year.'

'I see.' He studied her keenly for a moment before going on, 'I understand you have no immediate plans. I wonder, would you consider working in Switzerland?'

The suggestion took her breath away. 'Oh! I—it sounds attractive.'

'You probably know that I am retiring from my work here at the end of the year,' he continued. 'I shall be taking a more active part in a private clinic I'm connected with, not far from Lausanne. A fair number of our patients are English-speaking. I've been asked to recommend some British-trained nurses to fill a couple of gaps we have. I'm sure you would suit us very nicely. Would you like to think about it?'

He flashed her one of his paternal smiles, rising before she could reply. 'Do come and see me at my Kensington address if you'd like to know more. Shall we say tomorrow evening, about nine?' With a gracious nod he went on his way, leaving Bryony with her head in a whirl.

A private clinic in Switzerland? She wanted to put distance between herself and Grant Stirling, didn't she? What better solution could there be?

Private nursing paid well, too, and she couldn't really afford to be out of a job indefinitely. Not that she had ever considered working abroad, but there was nothing to be lost by going to see what it was all about.

Back at her flat that night Mike Tavistock phoned her. 'Hi, there, Light of my Life! Sorry I couldn't ring you back after you phoned. I was tied up.'

'I gathered,' said Bryony. 'It wasn't anything important . . . but something did crop up today.' She began by telling him of her decision to leave the Heathside.

'Hey, you can't do that,' he interrupted, 'I'll have no shoulder to cry on.'

'Oh, belt up and listen,' she laughed, going on to talk about her chat with Sir Phineas and the proposed interview. 'But I can't remember how to get to his place in Kensington. Will you give me directions?'

'No problem . . . I'll run you there,' Mike promptly offered. 'Sounds interesting. I'll pick you up at eight-thirty, okay?'

'Thanks. You're a pal,' returned Bryony. 'Sure it won't be hampering your love-life?'

He chuckled. 'It happens to be going rather well at the moment.'

'Mike, you're a shocker!'

'I don't suppose you're in the picture, are you?'

'About what?'

'Tell you tomorrow,' he returned mysteriously.

She replaced the receiver wishing her own life were running as smoothly as Mike's appeared to be.

The following evening he was there to collect her, as promised.

'So you caught the great man's eye,' he teased, heading the Spitfire in the direction of Kensington. 'Lucky for me Vivien isn't qualified yet or he might be whipping her off just as our affair is getting going.'

Bryony didn't comment, not wanting to be a bore. After all, she had said her piece once and if Mike hadn't a conscience about the matter, that was his affair.

'What was it that you were being so mysterious about last night when we spoke?' she asked.

'The Kensington set-up, my love. Phinny is Vivien's guardian, her uncle, actually.'

Bryony's eyes widened. 'Oh! I see.' Or she thought she did. Was that why Grant was so interested in her? Perhaps it was a convenient arrangement between himself and Sir Phineas.

'Well connected, our Vivien,' Mike went on. 'Luckily I was chasing her long before I discovered that fascinating fact, so she knows I'm not crawling.'

'Quite the little Sherlock Holmes, aren't you? Bryony said. 'How did you find out?'

'Viv told me. In confidence, of course. But I know you won't talk. She doesn't want it put around because she prefers to make it on her own merits; to be accepted for herself alone, sort of thing.' He sighed ecstatically. 'I think she's tremendous, as well as being a bobby-dazzler.'

'Doesn't she have any parents, then?'

Mike shook his head. 'Lost them both when she was a kid.'

Bryony was still trying to work things out. 'Where does Grant Stirling fit in? He's very thick with Sir Phineas, isn't he?'

'I drew a blank there. Give me time.' Mike parked in the square of graceful Georgian houses. 'But I don't see him as any great threat. Married to the job, isn't he?' He switched on his car radio and stretched. 'Ready? Off you go then, and good luck. I'll be here waiting.'

The conversation with Mike had given Bryony no time to think about being nervous, but waiting on the doorstep after ringing the bell above the polished brass plate, her stomach began to feel fluttery.

She was admitted by Sir Phineas's secretary, a softly-spoken Scotswoman. Ushering Bryony into a cosy sitting-room with an exquisite Chinese silk carpet on its polished boards, she introduced her to the other occupant of the room, a girl of about her own age.

'Miss Clemence, this is Miss Keane, who has also come about a position at the clinic.'

She poured them sherry and handed each girl an impressive-looking brochure, entitled The Schmidt-Forbes Clinic, Lausanne. 'Perhaps you would like to be looking through before Sir Phineas joins you.'

When she had left them the girls exchanged Christian names and other details as they sipped their drinks and studied the brochures. Teresa

Keane was from St Benedict's, a sister on an orthopaedic ward, Bryony learned.

It was welcome having a fellow nurse to discuss things with.

'If the pictures are anything to go by, this looks great,' Teresa said.

Flicking through the pages, showing the modern clinic buildings against their backdrop of snow-capped mountains and flowery meadows, Bryony had to admit that it certainly did look delightful.

'If everything else measures up, looks like we can't go wrong,' she agreed.

Sir Phineas arrived, impeccably dressed as usual, in a grey lounge suit. 'Sit down, my dears. Sit down,' he waved as they rose to greet him. 'How good of you to come.'

He proceeded to chat in an amiable way, stretching out in a fawn leather armchair opposite them, his bright eyes darting from one to the other as he expanded on the details in the brochure.

'We have one hundred beds, and two-thirds of those are single rooms. Two modern operating theatres, X-ray department, pharmacy, our own path lab, etcetera. We get our fair share of ski-ing accidents in the season. Then there are respiratory complaints, cardiacs, renal problems, a little plastic surgery; the usual kind of thing.'

'Where would we live? Bryony asked.

He turned a page in the brochure to point out a series of small chalets on a hillside, their balconies bright with window-boxes.

'We can provide you with accommodation in one

of these, I believe. Or sometimes people prefer to make their own arrangements in the village, once they are established.' He paused, waiting for their reactions.

'It sounds super,' said Teresa, beaming.

Bryony was a little less sure of herself, although she couldn't have said exactly why.

Noticing her slight hesitation, Sir Phineas went on: 'Of course, you will wish to discuss it with someone perhaps. And I'm not exactly *au fait* with details of things like leave and remuneration. If the job appeals to you, then you must meet my colleague, Professor Schmidt, and the Matron. That will also give you a chance to see the place for yourselves before you decide.'

He stroked his nose thoughtfully. 'I don't wish to hurry you, but we would wish you to start in the new year. Things get busy in January. When could you manage a visit. Tomorrow . . . the next day?'

'To Switzerland, you mean?' said Bryony.

The girls looked at each other and laughed.

'Yes. You can fly to Geneva in just over the hour. A short train ride from there to Lausanne, and a taxi from the station to the clinic. It's not difficult. You could do it in a day, but that might be a little tight. No, better stay overnight. We'll pay expenses, naturally.'

After a short discussion of their duty times, both girls agreed on Friday as being the first suitable day.

'Splendid!' said Sir Phineas, 'I'll get Miss Ross to come in and see you, to tie up the ends.'

He rose and left them and presently the secretary

reappeared to take particulars of their names and addresses in her notebook. She was also able to give them a few more factual details about the clinic than the rather vague picture outlined to them by the consultant.

'I'll try to get you on an early flight on Friday,' she promised, 'and I'll probably send the tickets round by hand to your wards, since time is short. But that's Sir Phineas,' she smiled, 'never lets the grass grow under his feet.' Bidding them a pleasant goodnight as she saw them off the premises, she said: 'Oh, by the way, you will of course take proof of your qualifications, and if you could put on paper a summary of your nursing careers, that would be helpful.'

Outside in the Square the girls lingered talking for a moment, both bowled over by the suddenness of events. They exchanged telephone numbers.

'I'll give you a ring after we get the info,' promised Teresa. 'My car's over there. How are you getting back?'

'A friend of mine gave me a lift; he's waiting for me.' With renewed promises to keep in touch, Bryony parted company with her new acquaintance and went back to Mike's car.

He was still listening to the radio but switched it off as she climbed in beside him. 'Well, how was it?'

Trying to sound enthusiastic, she told him all about it on the homeward journey.

'I should imagine you're onto a winner there,' he prophesied, 'but do I sense the tiniest bit of doubt?'

She wrinkled her nose. 'Oh, that's just me being

a stick-in-the-mud. What with losing Judy, and the idea of leaving my nice familiar scene, I'm all mixed up these days.'

Outside the flat Mike declined to come in. He kissed her a fond goodnight. 'Forward march, baby. There's a whole new world out there waiting to be discovered.'

'Thought you wanted my shoulder to cry on?'

He winked. 'I'm not aiming to do that much crying.'

# CHAPTER NINE

ON Wednesday afternoon at the conclusion of the doctors' round on Addison ward, Grant Stirling was able to discharge Mr Gladwin.

With a satisfied smile, Grant took leave of his patient. 'Just walk sometimes instead of using the car, Mr Gladwin, and watch your weight. We don't want to see you back in here.'

John Dawson also added his parting advice: 'Let other people do the rushing . . . you take it a bit easy.'

'You bet I will,' returned Mr Gladwin cheerfully. 'Thanks to all of you I've been given a breather, and I'm going to make the most of it. I was a lucky old geezer to get landed here, I reckon.' His grateful smile embraced them all.

Bryony accompanied the two doctors from the ward. 'Good to have a satisfied customer,' she said.

Grant gave her a keen, sideways glance from beneath his dark brows. 'And is that right that you'll soon be in line for the farewell dunking ceremony?' he asked, his resonant voice playing the usual havoc with her emotions.

She was taken aback that the news had leaked out so soon. Apart from the immediate people concerned, as yet she had mentioned it to no-one

other than Mike. 'We-ell,' she answered with a
fleeting smile, 'that doesn't happen to apply to
sisters. But how did you hear? The old grapevine, I
suppose.'

John grinned. 'Me, I'm afraid. Judy told me.'

'What are you going to do?' Grant prompted.

'Nothing's confirmed yet. But I daresay the
grapevine will get the information almost as soon as
I know myself.'

'Then I shall have to keep my ear to the ground,'
Grant said. He turned to John Dawson. 'I'll catch
you up on Simpson. I'm just going to have a quick
word with the anorexic girl. Her day out seemed
quite successful, don't you think, Bryony?'

She nodded. 'As far as we can tell there were no
hassles.'

'Then I see no reason why we shouldn't repeat
it.'

As Grant left them, John paused to apologise to
Bryony in case he'd spoken out of turn about her
resignation. 'Did I put my foot in it? Sorry.'

'It doesn't matter, John,' she assured him. 'It was
bound to come out. I should have known better
than to think I could quietly disappear from this
place.' But she was relieved to realise that he
apparently knew nothing of her interview with Sir
Phineas. She did not want people gossiping about
that until she had made up her mind what to do.

Sister McCullagh had returned from her tea-
break, bringing with her a bulky envelope addressed to Bryony and marked 'By Hand'. 'Here you
are, dear. The office asked me to bring this up.' She

looked curious, although there was nothing else on the envelope to indicate where it had come from.

With her senior newly back from days off there had been no chance so far for Bryony to make known her plans to Sister McCullagh. Now she decided she had better break the news before anyone else did so.

The older woman was surprised and obviously regretful. 'Oh, dear! You're leaving? And we've been getting on so well together.' She was nevertheless interested to hear what Bryony had in mind. 'Still, mustn't stand in the way of progress. What are you going to do?'

Bryony hesitated, but felt that with the packet in her hand it would be mean not to confide in Sister McCullagh, especially since she had been so nice to work with. 'Well, er . . .' she faltered, 'I was deciding to take a rest . . . go home for a bit. But then I met Sir Phineas, and he has asked me if I'd like to work in a Swiss clinic he's connected with. I'm going out to Lausanne on Friday, with a girl from St Benedict's, for an interview and to see the place. Exciting, isn't it?'

As she outlined the proposition she saw Sister McCullagh's genial expression fade to one of slight disapproval. 'Private nursing?' Her senior shrugged. 'It sounds glamorous, but I wouldn't care for it. They say some of these wealthy patients treat you like the hired help.'

Bryony had a distinct impression that Sister McCullagh was disappointed in her. 'People get sick and need looking after whatever their position in life,' she defended herself. 'Anyway, there's no harm in going to see what it's all about. I'm not obliged to accept.'

She had no time to study the contents of the package thoroughly before going off duty at four-thirty, but once back at the flat she was able to do so at her leisure. The air-ticket showed an early morning flight from Heathrow, arriving at Geneva at mid-day, and onward to Lausanne by train from the city air-terminal. The return flight arrived back at Heathrow at seven p.m. on the following evening. There was a covering explanatory letter from Miss Ross, enclosing a small supply of Swiss francs for her convenience.

Having searched through her diary for Teresa's telephone number, she was about to make the call when Teresa herself rang through. 'You've got your stuff, have you?' she asked, sounding full of excitement. 'I hope it doesn't prove to be a great big let-down after all the expense they've gone to. I mean, one would feel a bit awkward about not accepting . . .'

'I should imagine that anything Sir Phineas is connected with would be okay,' Bryony said and Teresa agreed with her.

They discussed what it would be best to wear, deciding that winter coats would be more correct for a business interview than informal gear.

'. . . and don't forget your passport,' Teresa added. 'I'll see you at the Swiss check-in desk then, about an hour before take-off. I'm going to ring my mother now. I haven't told them at home yet.'

Neither had Bryony told her family. It had been too late to put through a call the previous evening. She did so immediately after saying goodbye to Teresa, but strangely, for the first time in her life she felt reluctant to speak to them and she was not at all surprised at the reception her news was given.

'Private medicine? And in Switzerland? But why, darling?' her mother queried, nonplussed. 'Nothing's gone wrong at the Heathside, has it?'

'No, of course not,' returned Bryony in an over-bright voice. 'I'm fed up with the dreary old scene and this sounded like a fun opportunity, that's all.'

There was a pause at the other end of the line before her mother went on, 'But last time you were home everything was so wonderful on Addison ward. You didn't say a thing about wanting to leave. Of course, I know Judy's illness was upsetting for you, and now that she's got other plans, well, you're bound to feel lost for a while. That will pass, though. I think you were being too hasty, resigning. You've hardly had time to get yourself properly established as a sister yet.'

Bryony sighed and wished she could explain. Yet how could she say—It's not Addison, or the Heathside that I'm leaving. It's Grant Stirling.

Close as she was to her mother she could not bring herself to confide her hopeless yearning for Grant. Because even if Mike were successful in his play for Vivien, Bryony knew that she meant nothing at all to the registrar, except as the junior sister of Addison ward. And the more she tried to snap out of her obsession for the man, the more enamoured she seemed to get. It had become scarcely endurable to breathe the same air as him, knowing that antagonism was about the only emotion they shared.

'Oh well, I've never been to Switzerland,' Bryony reminded her mother casually. 'It'll be an interesting experience. I'll let you know what happens.'

Mike had already offered to drive her to the airport on Friday morning, but it was to be an early start and the journey was simple enough for her by Underground, especially since her only luggage would be an overnight bag. She decided there was really no need to bother him, but trying to get him on the phone at his flat in order to tell him so, proved impossible. She planned to see him at work the following day, but it was not until nine-thirty that night when she was going off duty that Bryony at last managed to catch up with him.

He had only just finished in theatre and was making rather wearily for the doctors' messroom when she grabbed him as he left the department.

'Okay, baby,' he said when she had explained, 'if you're sure you can manage, that's fine. But I'll come and meet you on Saturday. Mustn't neglect you, must I?'

He addressed a joking remark to someone who had come along behind her. 'You'll have to get yourself an understanding bird like Bryony, Grant.'

She turned and flushed to find herself in the way of the registrar. 'Sorry,' she murmured, standing to one side.

'And what is it she's being so understanding about?' he paused to enquire drily.

Mike put an arm around her shoulders and pecked her on the cheek. 'She's letting me off our early-morning assignation.' He stifled a yawn. 'Come and have a drink with us, Bryony?'

'No, thanks,' she returned quickly. 'I've rather a lot to do.'

Grant's mouth twisted. 'Don't let me frighten you away.'

'It's not an excuse, it happens to be true.' With a tight smile she said goodnight and left them.

'See you at Heathrow at seven on Saturday, then!' Mike called after her. 'Good luck!' and he went on with Grant.

Hurrying out to the car park, Bryony gritted her teeth. Mike and his clever remarks . . . she could have thrown things at him. And as for Grant, she boiled at his satirical tone of voice. How could you love and hate a person so much at one and the same time?

She started up her car in a plethora of agitation, narrowly missed hitting a smart Rover as she backed, and swore under her breath several times as she grated the gears before reaching the flat.

Doubtless by this time Grant would have learned about the position she was considering. Would he be as disapproving as Sister McCullagh and her mother? she brooded. Fortifying herself with a cup of tea, Bryony came to the conclusion that he'd most likely be so glad to see the back of her at the Heathside that he wouldn't care where she went. It was a depressing thought.

Well, here was her chance to get the man out of her system. And it wasn't as though she was planning permanent exile, she reflected, making an effort to be optimistic. Packing her overnight bag and getting her clothes ready for the morning, she managed to arouse some enthusiasm for the trip. She chose a pleated burgundy skirt and paler lambswool sweater to wear under her warm, white wool topcoat, with a colourful scarf to tie at her throat. Her natural suede high boots would complete the outfit.

Checking the Underground map she saw that it would be a fairly lengthy train journey to the airport and set her alarm accordingly, but the following morning she was up and bathing well before it rang. Not bothering with breakfast, she dressed carefully, popped passport and ticket-wallet into her shoulder bag, locked up the flat and set out for the station.

It was a damp, grey morning, with soggy leaves still littering the gutters, but a milk roundsman still whistled cheerfully as he clanked his crates around the half-awake streets. Bryony called in at a small corner shop for a newspaper, and the tousle-haired shopkeeper when she offered him a fifty-pence piece waved it aside:

'I got no change yet, my duck. You owe it to me.'

'Thank you,' Bryony smiled. 'I won't forget.'

She had seen the dark fellow in the ticket office on one or two occasions. He slapped down her ticket and gave her her change, saying: 'Where are you off to? On your holidays?'

'Wish I were,' she retorted with a grin.

The half-empty train rattled along with its cargo of early workers and travellers, speedily ticking off the stations. And Bryony's newspaper lay unopened on her lap as she watched the passing scene and realised how attached she had grown to the great metropolis and its people.

Arriving at Heathrow, she found Teresa already waiting for her at the Swiss check-in point. When their plane seats had been allocated they snatched a quick cup of coffee before making their way to the departure lounge, discussing the pro's and con's of private medicine and the charm of Sir Phineas once you got to know him.

Once aboard the DC9 they were quickly airborne, flying high above the clouds and across the English coastline, leaving behind, so Bryony felt, the most precious things in her life.

Teresa was a chatterbox, but Bryony was glad of her company. It prevented too much soul-searching. Even so, she found her attention wandering as the other girl rattled on about how this couldn't have come at a better time for her seeing that her romance had just petered out.

Buttering the hot croissants which had been served to them, her mind skipped back to hot breakfast rolls in that bedroom she had shared with Grant at the Leaping Stag Inn. She recalled the strength of his muscled body and the fierceness of his forceful kiss when she had tried to hit him. Yet he could be so gentle and solicitous. When Judy had been ill he had been kindness itself. There had certainly been a softness in his manner towards her a few nights previously, when they had dined at the King's Hotel, until she had somehow managed to spoil it all.

Oh, if only things could have been different between them! If they could have been friends even. It was galling to see how easily he talked with all the other nurses, and they adored him. Yet with Bryony it was as though a grille dropped down between them at the first hint of contact.

She sighed, reminding herself that it was a waste of time to worry about it, since it was probably true what Mike had said, even if there had been no Vivien. Grant was really dedicated to one thing only . . . his work.

'You want more coffee, Bryony?' Teresa interrupted her conversational flow while the air-hostess filled up their cups. Then she carried on: 'As I was saying, I came through Geneva last year on the way to Montreux for my spring holiday. That's at the other end of the lake. It's Lake Léman really, you know, although it's often called Lake Geneva. I've never actually been to Lausanne, though.'

They passed up their breakfast trays and Bryony searched in her shoulder-bag for the small travel booklet which she had bought in the hospital book-shop.

'There's a paragraph about it in here.' She turned

the pages. 'Here we are. It's a large, busy city, much like any other, I should imagine, except that it apparently straggles up and down steep hillsides. There's a university, museums, skyscrapers, and an older part around a Gothic cathedral, which looks rather handsome.'

She passed the booklet over for Teresa to see the pictures. 'Oh yes, and there's the funicular going down to the lake at Ouchy. I passed that when I went on a steamer trip,' Teresa remembered.

'The place we're going to is right up past the city, isn't it? Nice and rural, I hope. Cowbells in the meadows and all that.'

'Not too far from civilisation though,' said Teresa, 'and the public transport system is very efficient.'

The meal-trays had scarcely been cleared away before the plane started its descent. Looking out of the aircraft window as she fastened her seat-belt, Bryony glimpsed the vast panorama of snowclad summits and green hills and valleys dotted with tiny dwellings and ribboned with silver streams. Soon they were dropping into a mountain-ringed valley and crossing the vast, shimmering crescent of Lake Léman. As the plane skimmed a stand of trees and roared down onto the tarmac, Bryony felt a surge of excitement.

With only their hand luggage to think about the girls were soon through Customs and out into the crystal light of a Swiss December day. It was comparatively mild for the time of year, and Bryony's first impression was one of brightness and freshness. Even the Customs officials in their grey-green uniforms seemed smarter and more pleasant than in other airports.

'Oh, look! A Christmas tree already!' Bryony exclaimed, pausing to admire the glittering specimen in the arrivals lounge. 'And doesn't everything look clean.'

Teresa was more concerned with the practical. 'Come on, this is the way.' She led Bryony in the direction of the airport bus which was to take them to the city terminal and railway station.

Once aboard the train Bryony had her first close-up look at the countryside with its backdrop of rugged grandeur. They sped along past vineclad slopes and water-side gardens, picturesque chalets and farmhouses, with constant views of the magnificent lake with its smart white steamers and yachts at anchor.

Teresa eagerly provided bits of information that she had gleaned on her previous visit, remembering the names of famous people who had lived around the lake. 'They'll be along with refreshments soon,' she went on. 'We ought to have something, unless we want to faint at the Professor's feet!'

After a memorable ride they arrived at the Lausanne terminal. Approaching the first taxi in line, they showed the address of the clinic to the roguish-faced young driver.

He nodded in understanding. 'Ah, *oui*! *Très bien*. I take you.'

It was something of a hair-raising ride. Passing through the bustling city, their driver took them

across a bridge which spanned a steep-sided valley.
From then on it was sharp bends and steep gra-
dients taken at breakneck speed as the taxi flew on
and up. And with every twist and turn there were
the mountains above, or the lake below, and small
hamlets nestling in quiet isolation.

A few miles out of the city they came to a
sheltered valley, its village spread around its own
small lake. A good road led up from the village to a
plateau backed by a pine forest. And here sprawled
the modern complex of the Clinique Schmidt-
Forbes, with its own lighted Christmas tree on the
broad patio outside the main entrance.

Their driver pulled up and threw out a hand to
indicate their arrival.

Sorting out the fare between them, the girls
alighted and he waved them a cheery farewell,
saying:

'Get better quick!'

'The way he was driving you'd think he got a
commission on customers!' remarked Teresa as the
taxi leapt forward and away down the hill.

Bryony chuckled. 'Didn't think we looked *that*
anaemic.'

They both stood for a moment admiring the
view.

'Well, there are my cows in the meadows,' nodded Bryony, looking towards a group grazing on
the hillside, bells clanking melodiously.

'And this is it, then,' said Teresa. They turned to
climb the shallow steps leading to the reception
area of the clinic.

The plate glass door slid back automatically on their approach. Inside, a profusion of lush potted plants gave the place the air of a five-star hotel.

A pleasant-faced girl with a braid of flaxen hair round her head sat behind a large modern desk. '*Bonjour!*' she greeted them, but switched to English on learning their business.

'Ah, yes! You are expected. Please to sit down a moment.' Motioning them towards comfortable lounge chairs, she made a telephone call and afterwards conducted them to a businesslike office, furnished with two desks and some hide-covered seats. 'Please to wait here. The Professor and Matron will be along presently.'

They were only kept a few minutes. Professor Schmidt, when he arrived, could not have been more different from Sir Phineas. He was short and thick-set with a round, jolly face and a wealth of bristling iron-grey hair. The Matron, accompanying him, was what Bryony's dad would have described as 'a fine figure of a woman', it crossed her mind.

When greetings had been exchanged, together with polite enquiries about their journey, Matron seated herself at one desk and Professor Schmidt at the other, to interview each girl in turn.

The Professor beamed at Bryony after perusing her qualifications and the introductory letter from Sir Phineas. 'So, you are sister on a medical ward at the Royal 'Eathside 'Ospital, Mees Clemence? I know it. A splendid place. I 'ope you will decide to join us. Matron will explain the business side of things, and she will arrange to show you what you wish.'

Exchanging places with Teresa, Bryony learned from the matron details of salary, hours, accommodation, leave, and the kind of service she would be expected to give. 'The proportion of nursing staff to patients is high here. Many of our patients are used to having staff at home; naturally they desire personal attention when they are ill. Otherwise nursing procedures are much the same as those you employ in hospital in your own country.

His interviews with both girls concluded, Professor Schmidt took his leave of them with a polite little bow, requesting that they would give their decision to Sir Phineas as soon as possible.

The matron glanced at her watch. 'I have an appointment this afternoon, but I will find someone to show you our working arrangements. First of all, I am quite sure you would like some tea,' she said briskly, and conducted them back to the reception area where she asked the girl on the desk to arrange it.

In the smart staff restaurant which overlooked the valley, a sprinkling of other members were also there, enjoying an afternoon break.

'Everyone looks happy enough,' Bryony remarked, her eyes on a carefree foursome at a table. She tried to picture herself in the all-white trouser suit of the nursing sisters. 'I've often thought trousers might be more convenient for our job.'

'All very well for you slim-Jims,' said Teresa,

'but not so good when you're always fighting the flab like me.'

Making a face, she helped herself to another piece of creamy gateau. 'If this is the standard of the grub, I'm going to have to find some will-power from somewhere.'

Reporting back to the reception desk, they were introduced to an English nurse named Mandy, who had been appointed to show them around.

'I love it here,' Mandy told them, taking them up in the lift to view some of the private rooms, 'and I've been here almost a year now.'

Bryony was suitably impressed by the amenities which were luxurious by hospital standards. Fittings and furnishings were in excellent taste with attractive decor and lighting, and all rooms had bathrooms ensuite and balconies angled to the sun. But in the beds were the same limbs under traction, the same drip attachments and oxygen in readiness, the same anxious faces as in any other hospital. 'Mmm,' she murmured, 'lovely. But I daresay you feel just as bad with lung cancer or liver failure here as anywhere else.'

They went on to see the technological departments, all very much as Sir Phineas had described, all with the most up-to-date equipment. The kitchens were a chef's dream and the meals served on dainty crockery.

Lastly they were shown the staff facilities and the centrally heated chalets at the rear of the clinic where staff could live if they wished.

'I share one of these with two other girls,' Mandy

told them. 'The job has got its good and bad sides, like most. 'We're nicely situated. You can get into Lausanne on the bus . . . gorgeous shops. And it's not too far from Geneva or Montreaux. There's a sports centre in the village. When the ski-ing season proper starts there's lots of nightlife. And we get to see a fair number of the beautiful people.'

It had grown dark by this time and they stood looking down at the lights twinkling in the village.

'Well, I'd better get back to my work,' Mandy went on. 'Putting you up for the night at the Alpenhotel, aren't they? I'll be off duty at nine. I'll come down and show you around the village, if you like?'

Arranging to call for them as soon as she could, she directed them down the road towards the village and the Alpenhotel.

With the darkness frost had come down and Bryony turned her coat collar up about her ears. Craggy peaks reared mysteriously against a star-studded sky as the two girls stepped out in the keen night air.

'Well, I've made up my mind,' Teresa declared. 'Nothing to fault, is there?'

'No,' Bryony had to agree, 'it all seems perfect.' But privately, questions plagued her. Did she really want to be part of this life . . . to dance attendance on the already privileged? At the back of her mind there lurked the memory of all those average mums and dads she had nursed; the Tina Vincents, the Colin Goddards and the Mr Gladwins of this world. What was it he had said . . . her voice was like a candle in the dark? But for heaven's sake, she wasn't the only nurse in the world, she reminded herself.

But even setting aside that aspect, always colouring her judgments was the ache in her heart for Grant. Much as it was painful to be near him and not be able to love him, it was equally painful to be away from him. She felt reluctant to cut herself off.

It had been a long and tiring day. Reaching the steep-roofed, rustic-balconied hotel where rooms had been reserved for them, it was a relief to be able to relax at last.

Bryony took a refreshing shower before joining Teresa to go down to the cosy dining-room. They both did full justice to a meal of delicious *fondue bourguignonne* followed by chocolate mousse.

As good as her word, Mandy arrived shortly after nine in the company of a male nurse, who proved good company. They all went along to the sports centre for a game of ten-pin bowling, ending up later in a friendly night spot with a crackling log fire and talking well into the night.

'I don't suppose you'll have too much time tomorrow,' Mandy said in parting, 'but try to have a look at Lausanne before you go back to Geneva. It's a super place.' Then she laughed. 'But what's the hurry? You'll have all the time in the world to see everything when you join us, won't you?'

# CHAPTER TEN

Bryony surfaced from under the cosy duvet and let her gaze wander over the pleasant Swiss hotel room with its traditional painted furniture and striped blue folk-weave curtains, and a misty water-colour of Lake Léman on the wall. It took her a moment to collect her thoughts. The whole trip had a faintly unreal quality about it.

This time yesterday morning she had been in London. Tonight she would be back there again. But for the moment, here she was in a Swiss village that seemed to have slipped out of the pages of a picture-book.

Pulling on her dressing-gown she opened the door leading to her wooden balcony and stepped out. There had been a slight sprinkle of snow in the night, just enough to beautify pine trees, roof tops and the tiny steepled church sitting peacefully in the early morning sunlight. It gave the place a Christmas card atmosphere. She stretched and breathed deeply of the invigorating clean air, and found herself thinking of the frail bronchitic lady who had taken Judy's bed at the Heathside.

The door of the adjoining bedroom opened and Theresa also came out onto her balcony.

'Hi!' called Bryony. 'Isn't it grand?'

Teresa hunched her shoulders, pulled her wrap

closer about her and ran her finger along the whitened edge of the balcony railing. 'Super! Make the most of it. I expect it's wet and soggy in London.'

'I was just wishing I could press a button and transport someone in my ward out here,' Bryony said. 'This ozone would do her the world of good.'

'And a few more besides.' Teresa yawned, patting her mouth with her hand. She glanced at her watch. 'Oh Lord, is that the time? Better get a move on, I suppose, or we shan't catch that bus Mandy told us about. See you for breakfast in about twenty mins, right?'

In the dining-room a choice of hot croissants, breads, jams or cheeses, with fruit juice and coffee awaited them, making a satisfying start to the day. After which, collecting their belongings the girls took leave of the jovial proprietor of the Alpenhotel and made for the village square, waiting for the bus by the quaint old clock-tower, as advised.

The bright yellow coach arrived exactly on time, full of talkative housewives and shoppers, some of whom greeted the new passengers with polite *bonjours*. Within half-an-hour they were being set down in the centre of Lausanne.

'Hope you've got a good head for direction,' exclaimed Teresa, gazing around in confusion at the busy scene, 'because I haven't.'

Bryony was also studying the lay of the land. In one direction were shops and great modern buildings, while in another ran the cobbled streets and

well-preserved houses of the old town. She pointed
to a group of spires etched against the skyline.
'That must be the cathedral, Notre Dame, and this
way down the hill, I remember, is the way we came
from the station. So as long as we can find our way
back there we'll be okay. What shall we do? See the
old town first and then have a prowl round the
shops?'

Teresa agreed, and leaving the busy modern
thoroughfare, they sauntered through narrow by-
ways where tall, straight houses were gay with
window-boxes, finding the cobbled market with its
flower and vegetable stalls, and coming at last upon
the stately cathedral. It was set amid sculptured
green lawns, its ornate spires, turrets and beautiful-
ly weathered stone catching the sunlight.

'Oh!' exclaimed Bryony, quite enthralled, 'Oh, I
wish I had my camera.'

'Buy a picture-postcard,' suggested Teresa, so
they did.

With time pressing on this occasion they could
not afford more than a brief glimpse inside before
retracing their steps towards the modern zone and
its splendid shops. Everywhere were seasonal window displays and decorations, and wonderful
assortments of ski-wear and après-ski clothes, and
the most amazing selection of caps and hats they
had ever seen. Teresa could not resist buying herself a scarlet pull-on. 'We're bound to need one
later on,' she decided.

The confectioners shops were equally irresisti-
ble. Bryony bought small boxes of hand-made

chocolates for her mother and Sister McCullagh, and she settled on a decorated cowbell full of pralines for her sister Joanne.

Finding themselves near the funicular, it was an easy few minutes' ride down to the lakeside, where a welcoming café on the tree-lined waterfront served them a belated lunch.

So fascinating was it sitting by the lake, watching the swans and ducks and wild geese, and admiring reflections in the water, that the rest of the after-noon slipped away before they knew it. In the end they had a mad scramble to catch the train back to Geneva and the terminal bus for the airport.

'Wow!' laughed Bryony, when at last they were settled in their seats on the plane for the flight home. 'What a whirlwind trip!'

'Yes, it seems a pity to be going back, now that we're here,' Teresa remarked. 'I'd just as soon be starting straight away instead of waiting for the new year.' She chattered on, saying how lucky they were to know Sir Phineas, and wasn't Mandy fun, and what a great social scene it promised to be.

Bryony's thoughts were racing ahead to murky London. 'We-ell, there are all sorts of things to tie up at home,' she said, 'and there's Christmas . . .'

But a tiny voice in her head was reminding her that there was also Grant. She really had tried to make herself forget him. But he was there all the time, capturing her thoughts on the slightest pre-text.

She sighed heavily. She could only hope that in time she would learn to get over him.

In just over an hour they were fastening seat-belts for landing again, flying over a London ablaze with lights, touching down at Heathrow on a damp, chilly evening.

'My brother is meeting me. Can we give you a lift?' Teresa offered.

'No, thanks all the same. I'm being met too,' Bryony told her.

Passing through Customs and into the arrivals area, Teresa spotted her brother almost immediately. She waved. 'There he is! I'll see you then, Bryony.'

Promising to keep in touch, the two parted company. Bryony scanned the waiting crowds, searching for Mike's dark-bearded countenance. She could not pick him out at once, but it was quite possible he had been delayed by traffic. She was debating where best to stand in order to be seen, when there was a light tap on her shoulder.

Spinning round with a welcome on her lips, she was stunned to silence to find herself looking into the grey-green eyes of Grant Stirling. Grant, in a well-worn tweed sports jacket and polo-necked sweater, corduroy jeans baggy at the knees. Grant with a shadow of beard darkening his chin and the waves easing back into his usually well-brushed hair. She had never seen him looking quite so workaday. Her inside flipped. Her impulse was to throw her arms around him.

'Oh! Hallo,' she exclaimed, her breath coming quickly, 'What are you doing here? Are you meeting someone?'

'Yes . . . you. Mike couldn't make it.' He spoke gruffly, as though he had been press-ganged into taking on the job.

Her impulse was to turn and run. She drew a long, steadying breath, aware that she had flushed. 'Oh! Well, I-I'm sorry you had to be troubled. I-I mean, I hope it hasn't put you out too much.' The words came out with a rush.

'We could hardly have had you waiting here indefinitely, could we?' he growled.

Privately she was cursing Mike for having put her in this situation. He *knew* how she felt about Grant; well, not the *true* state of her feelings, but about their friction. She wished he had left a message for her so that she could have gone home by Underground.

'He could have had me paged or something. I could have made my own way.'

'That would have been a flat homecoming after your exciting excursion. My car's in the multistorey. Would you like something before we go?'

'Not really, thank you.' All she wanted to do was to go away somewhere by herself and howl.

He took her overnight case from her. 'Well, if you don't mind, I could use a coffee. I came straight from an emergency at the hospital . . . hence the tatty gear.'

She realised how tired he was looking, and that in spite of probably having had to work all hours he had driven through the Saturday traffic for her benefit.

'Oh, I'm sorry. Yes, of course, let's have a drink.'

Taking her elbow he steered her through the crowds towards the restaurant. 'You find a table,' he said, handing her back her case, and he went off towards the counter.

She cleared a vacant table of dirty cups and saucers and waited nervously, focussing on the sight of his shapely head, bent over his hand as he sorted out coins at the pay desk. She waved to attract his attention when he returned with the two coffees.

Seating himself opposite her, he tipped brown sugar into black coffee, regarding her with disconcerting candour. 'Well?' he said at length.

'Well what?'

'Well, what have you been up to?'

She concentrated on opening her small pot of cream, dribbling it into her cup. 'I suppose you know all about the Swiss clinic, since you're a buddy of Sir Phineas.'

'Yes, we are old friends. In fact he's always been my mentor. But that doesn't guarantee him keeping me informed of all his affairs.'

Bryony vaguely recalled a remark of his on their unforgettable journey to Devon, when he had spoken of someone being a major influence in his life. At the time she had presumed he must have meant Vivien. Now she said: 'Was it he you meant when you talked about someone influencing your life?'

Grant nodded. 'But we're not talking about me

. . . we're talking about his influence on *you*. What have you decided?'

Idly she fingered a sugar packet, trying to keep her hand steady. 'About the clinic? It's a great opportunity.'

He leaned forward and laid a hand over hers, asking abruptly, 'But is it what you want?'

She pulled away sharply from this disturbing contact. 'I wish people would stop trying to tell me what to do,' she snapped. 'I can run my own life.'

'Can you? Sometimes other people know you better than you know yourself.'

'Indeed?' Lifting her eyes, she met his searching gaze squarely. 'And why should it be the right course for Sir Phineas and not for me?'

'Don't be stupid. There's no comparison. He's had a lifetime at the job. He's entitled to a bit of ease at this end of his career. Although I don't entirely approve of his decision. I'm something of a patriot.'

'You?' she scoffed. 'You left Australia to come over here.'

'I was born here,' he retorted. 'Wasn't my fault my parents emigrated. I've simply come back to my roots. And the Heathside can't spare people like you, Bryony.'

'That's ridiculous. Who's going to miss me?'

He startled her by saying: 'I should, for one. I should miss our skirmishes.'

'Too bad! In any case, if I don't accept this, I shan't be staying at the Heathside. I *hate* our skirmishes.' She found her eyes suddenly filling with tears. 'Oh God! Can't we get out of here?' Fumbling for a handkerchief in her pocket, she gulped back a sob.

'I'm sorry. I didn't mean to upset you.'

Grant was *sorry* for upsetting her? Even through her embarrassed confusion the idea struck her as something of a novelty. Whatever had come over the man? Dabbing at her eyes, she sniffed and managed to regain her composure.

He finished his drink and rose, taking her by the arm to lead her in the right direction. In silence they made their way towards the lift for the car park. On reaching the right level he guided her to where his silver Talbot gleamed in a shadowy corner. But instead of unlocking the car at once, he leaned nonchalantly against it, subjecting her to a steady scrutiny.

'What is this all about, Bryony . . . flight instead of fight?'

'I don't know what you mean,' she returned levelly, despite the panic in her breast.

'Oh yes, I think you do. We both do.'

Her heart was beating so fast it hurt. 'Is this what your psychologist friend made of things?' she challenged, 'Because . . .'

'My dear girl,' he interrupted, 'just shut up and listen to me. I knew damn well why I fought with you. It didn't need a psychologist to tell me that. My problem was . . . how did *you* feel about *me*, hm?' He lifted her chin so that she could not escape from his probing gaze. 'Is it just the skirmishes you hate? Not me?'

Her eyes widened in amazement. What was he actually trying to tell her? 'N-no,' she faltered, 'I . . . I . . . hate is a strong word.'

'So is love. Would you be confusing the two emotions?' And then his mouth closed on hers in a gentle seeking kiss; a kiss that grew more urgent by the minute when it became obvious that he was meeting with no resistance, that she was a willing prisoner in his arms.

'My darling girl, couldn't you guess?' he murmured with his lips still close to hers, 'Couldn't you guess that I've been going crazy with love for you?'

The words sang in her ears. A wild surge of joy raced through her veins. She could hardly believe it. 'Oh Grant, how could I know? You've been so beastly to me sometimes.'

He held her very close. 'Forgive me for that. After what my mother did to my father, I misguidedly decided not to get entangled with women. That was until I met you. I fought you as long as I could,' he admitted.

His remarks woke her up to realities. There was still Vivien! Could it be that Grant had been using her to keep in with Sir Phineas? And now that the consultant was about to leave it was no longer necessary? She couldn't credit him with such callous behaviour. Disentangling herself from his arms, she stared at him stark-eyed. 'What about Vivien?'

'Vivien? Ah, yes.' He stroked his chin thoughtfully, then seemed to make up his mind about something. 'Let's go. There's someone I want you to meet.'

Sliding into the car alongside him, she could still scarcely believe that all this was not some mad flight of fancy on her part. Had Grant really said he loved her? Who did he want her to meet? And had he quarrelled with Vivien, or had they just decided to split?

'Where are you taking me?' she asked, her eyes fixed on him in a kind of wonder as he backed the car and followed the arrows down to the exit.

He grinned mysteriously, heading in the direction of London. 'You'll see.'

'Supposing Mike hadn't been working tonight,' she said presently, 'should I have left the Heathside without . . . without us . . . without you ever telling me?'

They had paused at some traffic lights. He took her hand and dropped a kiss on her palm. 'I didn't say Mike was working,' he said.

'Do you mean . . . you cooked this up between you? And after all you've said about him?'

Grant smiled. 'I'm always ready to bow to your better judgment.'

'You're not taking me to see Sir Phineas, are you?' She frowned, suddenly anxious, because her plans for the future were now in utter chaos.

'No. That will come later.'

There was so much she was in the dark about. 'You really are quite thick with him, aren't you? How did you actually meet?'

'During those school holidays I told you about.

He was the brother of my mother's second husband. He was always very good to me. But I'm not answering any more of your questions,' he went on. 'You tell me about your trip.'

By the time she had described the clinic, and gone into ecstasies over the delights of Lausanne in particular and Switzerland in general, they had arrived back at the block of flats where Grant, and also Mike, lived.

'Are we going to your place?' Bryony asked.

'No, to Mike's.' Inside the lift as they travelled up he pulled her to him, dropping small glad kisses on her face, so that she wished the ride could go on forever.

Arriving at the third floor he took her hand and walked her along the corridor to Mike's rooms, where he rang a peremptory blast on the bell.

'Oh, hi! So you found her,' beamed a jubilant Mike when he let them in.

There were sounds of activity from his kitchen and in a moment a pink-cheeked Vivien emerged, cooking spoon in hand, a tea-towel pinned around her jeans.

Grant went over to kiss her and beckoned to Bryony: 'Come here and meet my half-sister.'

Bryony's eyes popped. 'Your—half-sister?'

Vivien creased into giggles. ''Fraid so. Grant saw me as some kind of protection against predatory females, that's why we didn't let on. Nut-case, isn't he? But he reckoned without falling for you.'

Mike was pouring drinks and he handed one to Bryony, standing there with her head in a whirl. 'So you see, old thing, wasn't forbidden territory, was it?' he winked.

'H-how long have you known?' she demanded.

'Not too long, about that. I haven't been holding out on you, sweetie,' he assured her. 'But you've worked out the tie-up with Phinny now, haven't you?'

Bryony's brain was still reeling. 'No, not exactly.'

Grant took it upon himself to explain. 'After our mother died, Phinny was determined that we two kids shouldn't lose touch. He felt it his duty to keep us together since he's getting on in years and apart from himself, Vivien has no-one else except me.'

'And me now, don't forget,' put in Mike stoutly.

Vivien wrinkled her nose at him. 'Better get back to my kitchen, I suppose. I'm doing my famous chicken risotto. We could stretch it to four, if you'd like to stay and have some?'

'Not this time, thanks,' Grant said. 'We've other plans . . . after I've got myself cleaned up a bit. We'll push off and leave you to it.'

The door of Mike's flat closed behind them. Grant put his arm around Bryony, heading for the lift again. 'Come upstairs with me while I put my shaver over these whiskers?'

She nodded and managed to contain herself until they reached the privacy of his apartment. Then she exploded. 'Well! Of all the devious, underhand, two-faced creatures, you're the absolute end.'

He suppressed a grin. 'You jumped to your own

conclusions. I never said that Vivien and I were . . .'

'No, but you let me think . . .' she interrupted, 'and I went through hell, you louse!' She clenched her fists to beat on his chest again, but once more he pinned her hands behind her with his superior strength.

'Careful! Remember what happened to you last time you attacked me?'

She smiled slowly, and then laughed. 'Perhaps I wouldn't object now.'

He released her and passed a hand over his stubbly chin. 'I think you'd better wait . . . I don't want to inflict my bristles on you.'

'And I thought you didn't approve of Mike?' she challenged.

Grant shook his head. 'I guess my real quarrel with Mike was his closeness to you. He turned up trumps tonight, didn't he? Give me five minutes, my darling,' he said, lightly ruffling her hair. 'Make yourself at home.' He disappeared into the bathroom.

Bryony slipped off her coat and smoothed her rumpled locks. Looking around the cluttered living-room, she piled up the scientific papers and books which littered the floor around the divan, took a used tumbler and coffee mug out to the kitchen, and came back to study some family photos sitting on top of his bureau.

'What were these other plans we're supposed to have for tonight?' she called when the noise of the electric shaver had ceased.

He came from the bathroom bare-chested, mopping his face with a towel.

'I thought we might go to the King's Head again for supper . . . if you promise not to do another strip-tease. We can talk about plans while we're there.' Slinging the towel about his shoulders, he clasped his hands around her waist. 'For instance, you won't be taking that job in Switzerland, will you?'

He rested his nose against hers. She could smell the fresh tang of soap on his skin.

'It's a beautiful country,' she murmured.

'What about for a honeymoon?'

'Perfect for a honeymoon.'

With that, he gathered her, unresisting, against the controlled power of his body, kissing her so deeply that she felt she would drown with joy.